GA**WIRR**SIPOVICI was born in Nice in 1940 of Russo-Ital **Plea**ano-Levantine parents. He lived in Egypt from 1945 **last (** when he came to Britain. He read English at St Edm **re'** l, Oxford, graduating with a First in 1961. From 1963 he taught at the University of Sussex. He has publi——ver a dozen novels, three volumes of short stories and a **site** er of critical books. His plays have been performed throu : Britain and on radio in Britain, France and Germ and his work has been translated into the major Euro{ anguages and Arabic. In 2001 he published *A Life*, a biogr 1 al memoir of his mother, the translator and poet Sacha inovitch (London Magazine editions). His most recent ks are *Two Novels: 'After' and 'Making Mistakes'* (Carcanet) and *W Ever Happened to Modernism?* (Yale University Press).

Also by Gabriel Josipovici

Fiction
*The Inventory* (1968)
*Words* (1971)
*Mobius the Stripper: Stories and Short Plays* (1974)
*The Present* (1975)
*Four Stories* (1977)
*Migrations* (1977)
*The Echo Chamber* (1979)
*The Air We Breathe* (1981)
*Conversations in Another Room* (1984)
*Contre Jour: A Triptych after Pierre Bonnard* (1987)
*In the Fertile Land* (1987)
*Steps: Selected Fiction and Drama* (1990)
*The Big Glass* (1991)
*In a Hotel Garden* (1993)
*Moo Pak* (1995)
*Now* (1998)
*Goldberg: Variations* (2002)
*Everything Passes* (2006)
*Two Novels: 'After' and 'Making Mistakes'* (2009)

Theatre
*Mobius the Stripper* (1974)
*Vergil Dying* (1977)

Non-fiction
*The World and the Book* (1971, 1979)
*The Lessons of Modernism* (1977, 1987)
*Writing and the Body* (1982)
*The Mirror of Criticism: Selected Reviews* (1983)
*The Book of God: A Response to the Bible* (1988, 1990)
*Text and voice: Essays 1981-1991* (1992)
*A Life* (2001)
*The Singer on the Shore: Essays 1991-2004* (2006)
(ed.) *The Modern English Novel: The Reader, the Writer and the Book* (1975)
(ed.) *The Siren's Song: Selected Essays of Maurice Blanchot* (1980)
(ed. with Brian Cummings) *The Spirit of England: Selected Essays of Stephen Medcalf* (2009)

GABRIEL JOSIPOVICI

*Heart's Wings*
*&*
*other stories*

**CARCANET**

First published in Great Britain in 2010 by
Carcanet Press Limited
Alliance House
Cross Street
Manchester M2 7AQ

ISBN 978 1 84777 006 6

The publisher acknowledges financial assistance from Arts Council England

Supported by
ARTS COUNCIL
ENGLAND

Typeset in Monotype Centaur by XL Publishing Services, Tiverton
Printed and bound in England by SRP Ltd, Exeter

*For Tamar*

# Acknowledgements

Many of these stories were first published in anthologies and journals. I am grateful to the editors and publishers for allowing me to reprint:

'Second Person Looking Out' in *New Stories I*, ed. Margaret Drabble and Charles Osborne (Arts Council of Great Britain, 1976); 'Mobius the Stripper' in *Penguin Modern Stories 12*, ed. Judith Burnley (Penguin Books, 1972); 'The Bird Cage' was first read on BBC Radio 3; 'Waiting' in *Quarto*; 'Memories of a Mirrored Room in Hamburg' in *New Stories 5*, ed. Susan Hill and Isabel Quigly (Arts Council of Great Britain, 1980); 'He' in Gabriel Josipovici, *Four Stories* (Menard Press, 1977); 'Brothers' in *Nouvelle Revue Française* (in French translation) and *The Jewish Quarterly*; 'That Which Is Hidden...' and 'Steps' in *The London Review of Books*; 'A Changeable Report' in *Shakespeare Stories*, ed. Giles Gordon (Hamish Hamilton, 1982); 'Volume IV, pp. 167–69' and 'Exile' in *Comparative Criticism*, ed. Elinor Schaffer (Cambridge University Press, 1984); 'In the Fertile Land' and 'The Two Lönnrots' in *PN Review*; 'A Modern Fairy Tale', in *Caught in a Story: Contemporary Fairy-Tales and Fables*, ed. Christine Park and Caroline Heaton (Vintage, 1992); 'Donne Undone' (under the title 'Can More be Done?') in *God: An Anthology of Fiction*, ed. Stephen Hayward and Sarah Lefanu (Serpent's Tail, 1992); 'The Hand of God' in *The Slow Mirror and Other Stories: New Fiction by Jewish Writers*, ed. Sonja Lyndon and Sylvia Paskin (Five Leaves Publications, 1996); 'A Glass of Water' in *Modern Painters* (Winter 2000); 'Heart's Wings' in *Ovid Metamorphosed*, ed. Philip Terry (Chatto & Windus, 2000); 'Tegel' in *The Jewish Quarterly*; 'Christmas' in German in *Das Wüste Wilde Weihnachtsbuch*, ed. Gerd Haffmans (Zweitausendeins, 2003); 'Love Across the Borders' in German in *Der Rabe* (Zweitausendeins, 2007).

# Contents

# Second Person Looking Out

## I

— In the house, says my guide, there are seventeen rooms. And each room has three windows, which can be moved to any position on the walls or covered over if necessary.

— Is it a temple? I ask, hurrying to keep pace with him. Although he does not appear to walk fast his pace is deceptive.

— No no, my guide says. A private house.

The path is narrow and winds round hillocks and down into little valleys before plunging again into thick woods. My guide does not wait for me or make any concessions to my lack of experience of the terrain. He moves forward without effort, throwing the words back over his left shoulder.

— If you go from one room to another, he says, the head of the house, your host, may move a window fractionally along the wall or transplant it to another wall altogether, so that when you return to the first room you see another landscape outside, differently framed.

Inside the house people stand in tight groups, drinking champagne out of long-stemmed glasses and talking loudly. I stand at the window, looking out.

— What you experience as you approach the house, my guide says, is very important. First you may see a little bit of the house, then it disappears for several minutes, then you see another aspect of it, because the path is winding gradually round it. And when you finally reach it, because you are constantly seeing fragments of it and imagining it when you can't see it, you've experienced it in a million forms, you've already lived in the house, whole dramas have occurred before you even reach it, centuries have elapsed and you are still as far away from it as ever.

The path is narrow, so that it is impossible for the two of us to walk abreast. At times I have to break into a run to keep up with him.

— How far is it still? I ask him.

— We will soon be there, he says.

We trudge through the thick trees. The sky is invisible from here and it is impossible to tell the time of day. My guide has explained to me: — When you leave the house many of the paths will be barred to you. A small bamboo stick will be placed across the path. Do not try to cross the bamboo sticks. Retrace your steps. Follow the stones which have a piece of string tied round them and fastened in a triple knot.

— Excuse me, someone says. It is a white-coated waiter with a tray of long-stemmed glasses filled to the brim with sparkling champagne. I take a glass from the tray.

— The house, my guide says.

I look through the trees but can see only hills beyond and then more trees beyond that.

— Where? I ask him.

— We can no longer see it, he says. Please pay attention and look at once when I tell you.

He is a small stocky man with an even stride. He walks

without stopping or looking back at me.

As we come round the edge of a hillock I see a light in the distance. — Is that it? I ask him.

He hurries on ahead of me.

— Is that the house? I ask again.

— That is the house.

It has disappeared again. We are walking across open heath-land. The sky is quite blue overhead.

— The heath you see over there, the waiter says, pointing with his chin, that is where they will come from.

— Who? I ask him.

— He turns away. I stretch out my hand and take a glass from his tray. I wander into another room.

I have been in this room before, but the windows have been moved. Now, instead of three windows on the one wall, all looking out over the same prospect, there is only one on that side and two on the wall opposite.

— It is the habit of the house, my host explains, showing me round. The windows are moved once a guest has looked through them.

— That must be disconcerting for the guest, I say, laughing.

— It is the habit, he says.

He stands beside me, looking out over the darkening land-scape. — A guide is given for the return journey, he says. Never for the journey here.

— I came with a guide, I say.

— In that case, he says, it was the return journey.

People are pressing into us on all sides, talking and laughing. My host says: — To find your way out you follow the stones that have a piece of string tied round them and fastened with a triple knot.

I am in another room. My host has gone. I stand, looking out of the window.

Suddenly my guide says: — Over there. I look up quickly and true enough, the house is visible once more, very close now, though still somewhat masked by the trees.

— We must be almost there, I say.

But the path must wind away from the house because the next time it appears it seems to be a good deal further off.

— But when do we arrive? I ask my guide.

— We have arrived, he says.

— No no, I say. I mean the house itself. Not just the grounds.

— The distinction is meaningless, he says, hurrying on.

The waiter returns with the tray of champagne. My host takes one of the glasses and hands it to me. He himself already has a half-empty glass in his hand.

— Welcome! he says.

— Why do you welcome me now, I say, when we have already been talking for some time?

He shrugs. — It is the custom, he says.

I turn back to the window. It has disappeared.

— It is done with screens, my host explains. Paper screens.

He adds: — Shall we move into the next room? There are people there I would like you to meet.


## II


He has walked through the seventeen rooms. He has talked to many of the guests as well as to his host. At times he has stopped alone in front of a window and stared out at the landscape.

It has been explained to him that the house is approached by numerous paths. Some of them, he has been told, will be closed when he leaves, but, by following those stones which have a piece of string tied round them and fastened in a triple knot, he will be able to find his way out.

— How much further is it? he asks his guide.

— Not much further, the man says, hurrying ahead.

They round a hillock and there is the house, ahead of them.

— There are seventeen rooms in the house, the guide explains. Each room has three windows, which can be moved to any position on the walls or covered over if necessary.

His host has moved away from him and wandered into the next room. The young lady to whom he has just been introduced asks him: — Is this a temple or something?

— No, he says. Just a private house.

— It reminds me of a temple, she says.

They are standing in the fourteenth room. The three windows all face the tall trees at the back of the house. The light from the downstairs rooms illuminates the lawn, but that only serves to emphasise the darkness that reigns under the trees. His host, in answer to a question, explains: — The windows are always moved once a guest has looked through them.

— That must be disconcerting for the guests, he says.

— It is the custom, his host says, standing beside him in the dark.

He advances slowly, feeling each step ahead of him for fear of treading on a bamboo stick laid across the path. Every now and again he lights a match and holds it close to the ground, looking for the stones which have a piece of string tied round them and fastened in a triple knot.

— Do temples have to be holy? the girl asks him. I mean, she

adds laughing, couldn't people be having a party in a temple or
something?

There are too many people in each room. They stand,
wedged together, holding their long-stemmed glasses and
talking. There is nowhere to sit down.

— I mean, the girl says, it would be original, wouldn't it, a
party in a temple?

His guide moves with even steps, always ahead. He throws
comments and instructions over his left shoulder, for the path
is too narrow for two people to walk abreast. — Don't lag, he
says. Look when I point.

The rooms are packed with people. He pushes his way
through, muttering apologies, looking for his host. Eventually
he finds him, on his own, by a window, looking out.

— It is time for me to leave, he says, bowing slightly and
bringing his hands together in front of his chest.

His host shrugs but does not answer.

— I have been into all the rooms, he says, and looked through
all the windows. I have talked to all the guests.

— There are always new guests, his host says, smiling. And
new positions for the windows.

— Nevertheless it is time for me to leave.

— Patience, his host says. Patience. Follow the stones which
have a piece of string tied round them and you cannot go wrong.

— Yes, he says, I will do that, don't worry about me.

— You have tried seventeen paths, his host says. Perhaps the
eighteenth will not be blocked.

They resume their slow progress through the dark trees.

— I am surprised you cannot direct me to the right path, he
says, stepping into the darkness.

His host laughs. — I can only counsel you, he says. You

would not want me to make your decisions for you, would you? He adds: — But it is highly unlikely that there are many more than eighteen paths.

They move forward again and a light comes into view, high up through the trees. It is a window of the house. Inside, the party still seems to be in progress. People crowd the room and a waiter in a white jacket circulates with a tray of long-stemmed glasses. A man stands alone at the window, looking out.

— Why eighteen? he asks.

— His host laughs again in the darkness beside him. — I don't know he says. Eighteen seems to be such a realistic number.

They start to walk down the eighteenth path.

— Goodbye, his host says, bowing formally from the waist and starting to back into another room. Thank you for coming. He adds: — A servant will show you to the door.

## III

You walk alone under the trees. You seek the path that will lead you out.

You follow the stones with the string tied round them and fastened in a tripe knot. When a bamboo stick is laid across the path you turn back and start again.

You know that by now you should be almost within reach of the house.

You move quickly from room to room, looking for your host.

You touch the stones, feeling in the darkness for the string.

— It is a private house, your guide says. Inside, a party is in progress. People stand in tight groups in each of the rooms sipping champagne and talking loudly. One or two stand at windows, looking out.

— That is the way you go when you leave, the girl to whom you have just been introduced explains to you. Her husband, it turns out, is in the diplomatic service. You have already had a long talk with him, but in another room.

— In a moment you will be there, your guide says.

You ask your host if the house has always belonged to his family.

— Good heavens no! he says. I wish it had, he adds, and laughs.

— Fifteen stones with string tied round them and fastened in a triple knot have followed each other in rapid succession. The path has grown broader. You light a match and hold it down close to the ground. Another stone comes into view. The string tied neatly round it gives it the appearance of a parcel waiting to be picked up.

You turn round to see how far you have come, but the path must have curved without your noticing and neither the house nor any of its lighted windows is anywhere to be seen.

— Should we not have arrived by now? you ask your guide.

— Keep on your toes, he says, and you are not sure if you are meant to take this literally or if he is simply using an expression he has picked up. When I give the word, he says, look up at once.

You look up. But where a moment before there was a window there is now only a blank wall.

— Don't be surprised, your host says. Even seventeen stones with string tied round them and fastened in a triple knot do not necessarily imply an eighteenth.

— No, you say, I suppose not. You move your foot forward

with care, feeling for the bamboo stick.

And sure enough the stick is there. Now that the position of the window has been altered you can just make it out, gleaming whitely under the trees at the turn in the path.

# Mobius the Stripper

*A topological exercise*

No one ever knew the origins and background of Mobius the Stripper. 'I'm not English,' he would say, 'that's for certain.' His language was an uneasy mixture of idioms and accents, jostling

---

I first heard of Mobius the Stripper from a girl with big feet called Jenny. She was one of those girls who make a point of always knowing what's going on, and in those days she was constantly coming up with bright and bizarre little items of information in which she tried to interest me. Once she dragged me to Ealing where, in the small and smoke-filled back room of a dingy terrace, a fakir of sorts first turned a snake into a rope, then climbed the rope and sat fanning himself with a mauve silk handkerchief with his greasy hair just touching the flaking ceiling, then redescended and turned the rope back into a snake before finally returning the creature to the little leather bag from which he had taken it. A cheap trick. Another time she took me to Greenwich, where a friend of hers knew a man who kept six seals in his bathtub, but the man was gone or dead or simply

each other as the words fell from his thick lips. He was always ready to talk. To anyone who would listen. He had to explain. It was a need.

— You see. What I do. My motive. Is not seshual. Is metaphysical. A metaphysical motive, see? I red Jennett. Prust. Nitch. Those boys. All say the same. Is a metaphysical need. To strip. To take off what society has put on me. What my father and my mother have put on me. What my friends have put on me. What I have put on me. And I say to me: What are you, Mobius? A man? A woman? A vedge table? Are you a stone, Mobius? This fat. You feel here. Here. Like it's folds of fat, see. And it's me, Mobius. This the mystery. I want to get right down behind this fat to the centre of me. And you can help me. Yes, you.

---

unwilling to answer her friend's urgent ring at the doorbell. Most of all, though, Jenny's interest centred on deviant sexuality, and she was forever urging me to go with her to some dreary nightclub or 'ned of wice' as she liked to call it, where men, women, children and monsters of every description did their best to plug the gaps in creation which a thoughtful nature had benevolently provided for just such a purpose. Usually I didn't respond to these invitations of Jenny's, partly because her big feet embarrassed me (though she was a likeable girl with some distinction as a lacrosse player I believe), and partly because this kind of thing did not greatly interest me anyway.

— But it *must* interest you, Jenny would say. They're all part of our world, aren't they?

I agreed, but explained that not all parts of the world held an equal interest for me. — I don't understand you, she said. You say you want to be a writer and then you *shut* your mind to expe-

Everybody can help Mobius. That the mystery. You and you and you. You think you just helping yourself but you helping me. And for why? Because in ultimate is not seshual. Is meta-physical. Maybe religious.

When Mobius spoke other people listened. He had pres-ence. Not just size or melancholy but presence. There was something about the man that demanded attention and got it. No one knew where he lived, not even the manager of the club in Notting Hill, behind the tube station, where he stripped in public, seven nights a week.

— You want to take Mondays off? Tony the manager asked when he engaged him.

— Off? Mobius said.

---

rience. You simply *shut* your mind to it. You live in an ivory bower.

I accepted what she said. My mistake was ever to have told her I wanted to be a writer. The rest I deserved.

— Did Shakepeare have your attitude? Jenny said. Did Leonardo?

No. I had to admit. Shakespeare had not had my attitude. Neither had Leonardo.

Sometimes, at this point, I'd be sorry for Jenny, for her big feet and her fresh English face. Mobius. Mobius the Stripper. I could just imagine him. His real name was Ted Binks. He had broad shoulders and a waist narrow as a girl's. When he walked he pranced and when he laughed he.

— Well then, Jenny repeated, as if my admission made further discussion unnecessary. I sighed and said:

— All right. I'll come if you want me to. But if we're going

— We allow you one night a week off, the manager said. We treat our artists proper.

— I doan understand, Mobius said. You employ me or you doan employ me. There an end.

— You have rights, the manager said. We treat our artists proper here. We're not in the business to exploit them.

— You not exploitin, Mobius said. You doin me a favour. You payin me and giving me pleasure both.

— All right, the manager said. I'm easy.

— You easy with me I easy with you, Mobius said. Okydoke?

— You're on at six this evening then, the manager said, getting up and opening the door of his little office.

Mobius wanted to kiss him but the manager, a young man

---

to go all the way across London again only to find the door shut in our faces and the —

— That only happened once, Jenny said. I don't see why you have to bring it up like this every time. Anyway, it was you who wanted to see those seals. As soon as I told you about them you wanted to see them.

— All right, I said, resigned. All right.

— It's yourself you're doing a favour to, not me, Jenny would add at this point. You can't write without experience, and how the hell are you going to gain experience if you stay shut up in here all day long?

Indeed, the girl had a point. She wasn't strictly accurate, since my mornings were spent delivering laundry for NU-nap, the new nappy service ('We Clean Dirt', they modestly informed the world in violet letters on their cream van — I used to wake up whispering that phrase to myself, at times it seemed

with a diamond tiepin, hastily stepped back behind his desk. When the door shut behind Mobius he slumped back in his chair, buried his head in his hands, and burst into tears. Nor was he ever afterwards able to account for this uncharacteristic gesture or forget it, hard as he tried.

Mobius arrived at five that afternoon and every subsequent afternoon as well. — You need concentration, he would say. A good stripper needs to get in the right mood. Is like yoga. All matter of concentration and relaxation.

— Yes, the manager would say. Yes. Of course. Of course.

— With me, Mobius explained to him, is not seshual, is metaphysical. A metaphysical motive. Not like the rest of this garbage.

---

to be the most beautiful combination of the most beautiful words in the language), and my evenings kicking the leaves in the park as I watched the world go by. But not quite inaccurate either since I recognised within myself a strong urge towards seclusion, a shutting out of the world and its too urgent claims, Jenny included. And not just the world. The past too I would have liked to banish from my consciousness at times, and with it all the books I had ever read. As I bent over my desk in the afternoons, staring at the virgin paper, I would wish fervently, pray desperately to whatever deity would answer my prayers, that all the print which had ever been conveyed by my eyes to my brain and thence buried deep inside me where it remained to fester could be removed by a sharp painless and efficient knife. Not that I felt history to be a nightmare from which I wanted to awake, etcetera etcetera, but simply that I felt the little self I once possessed to be dangerously threatened by the

But they didn't mind him saying that. Everybody liked Mobius except Tony the manager. The girls liked him best. — Hi Moby, they said. How's your dick?

— Is keeping up, he would say. How's yours?

They wanted to know about his private life but he gave nothing away. — We're always telling you about our problems, they complained. Why don't you ever tell us about yours?

— I doan have problems, Mobius said.

— Come off it, they said laughing. Everyone's got problems.

— You have problems? he asked them, surprised.

— Would we be in this lousy joint if we didn't?

— Problems, problems, Mobius said. Is human invention, problems.

---

size and the *assurance* of all the great men who had come before me. There they were, solid, smiling, melancholy or grim as the case might be, Virgil and Dante and Descartes and Words-worth and Joyce, lodged inside me, each telling me the truth — and who could doubt that it was the truth, their very lives bore witness to the fact — but was it my truth, that was the question. And behind that, of course, another question: Was I entitled to a truth of my own at all, and if so, was it not precisely by following Jenny out into the cold streets of Richmond or Bermondsey or Highgate that I should find it?

At other times I'd catch myself before I spoke and, furious at the degree of condescension involved in feeling sorry for Jenny — who was I to feel sorry for anyone? — would say to her instead: — Fuck off. I want to work.

— Work later.

— No. I've got to work now.

But they felt melancholy in the late afternoons, far from their families, and in the early hours of the morning, when the public had all departed. — Where do you live? they asked him. — Do you have a man or a woman? Do you have any children, Moby?

To all these questions he replied with the same kindly smile, but once when he caught one of them tailing him after a show he came back and hit her across the face with his glove so that none of them ever tried anything like that again.

— I doan ask you you doan ask me, he said to them after the incident. I have no secrets but my life is my own business. And when Tony came to have a talk with him about the girl's disfigured cheek he just closed his eyes and didn't answer.

---

— It's good for your work. You can't create out of your own entrails.

— There are always excuses. It's always either too early or too late.

— You want to be another of those people who churn out tepid trivia because it's the thing to be a writer. Why not forget that bit and live a little for a change?

Dear Jenny. Despite her big feet — no, no, because of them — she never let go. She knew I'd give way in the end and if she'd come to me with the news in the first place it was only because she hadn't found anyone else to take her anyway. Jenny had a nose for the peculiar, but she was an old-fashioned girl at heart and felt the need of an escort wherever she went.

— Look, I said to her, I don't want to live, I want to be left in peace to work.

— But this guy, she said. The rolls of fat on him. It's fantastic.

— If it happens again you're out, Tony said, but although he would, in his heart of hearts, have been relieved had this in fact occurred, they both of them knew it was just talk. For Mobius was a goldmine. He really drew them in.

Alone in his little room, not many streets away from the club, he sat on the edge of the bed and stuffed himself sick on bananas. — Meat is meat, he would say. I'm no cannibal. Bananas he ate by the hundredweight, sitting with bowed shoulders and sagging folds of fat on the narrow unmade bed, staring at the blank wall.

Those were good hours, the hours spent staring at the wall, waiting for four o'clock. Not as good as the hours after four, but good hours all the same. For what harm was he doing? If

---

And the serenity. Everyone says you should see the serenity in his eyes when he strips.

— Serenity? I said. What are you talking about?

— It's like a Buddha or something, Jenny said.

— What are you trying to do to me? I said.

— Am I one of those people who fall for Zen and yoga and all the rest of that Eastern crap? Jenny said.

I had to admit she wasn't.

— I'm telling you, she said. It's a great experience.

— Another time, I said.

Cheltenham hadn't prepared her for this. Her eyes popped.

— Another time, I said again.

— You mean — you're not going to come?

— Another time, I said.

— Wow, Jenny said. Something must be happening to you, are you in love or something?

you don't pick a banana when it's ripe it rots, so again, what harm was he doing? Who was he hurting?

Sometimes the voices started and he sat back and listened to them with pride. – Who's talking of Mobius? he would say. I tell you, everybody's talking of Mobius. When I walk I hear them. When I sleep I hear them. When I sit in my room I hear them. Mobius the Stripper. The best in the business. I've seen many strippers in my time but there's none to beat Mobius. I first met Mobius. I first saw Mobius. I first heard of Mobius. A friend of mine. A cousin. A duchess, the Duchess of Folkestone. We had been childhood friends. I remember her remarking that Mobius the Stripper was the most amazing man she ever knew. I hear them all. But what do I care? That too

---

– I just want to work, I said.

– You always say that, Jenny said, suddenly deflated.

– I'm sorry, I said, and I was. Desperately. What sort of luck is it to be born with big feet? – Another time, I said. OK?

– You don't know what you're missing, Jenny said. True enough, but I could guess. Mobius the Stripper, six foot eight and round as a barrel. – That time Primo Carnera was chewing my big toe off. I couldn't get a proper grip on the slimy bastard so I grope around and he's chewing my toe like it'll come off any minute and then I find I've got my finger up his nostril and. Yes. Very good. He was another one I could do without.

After Jenny had gone I stared at the virgin sheet of paper on the table in front of me. When I did that I always wanted to scream. And when I left it there and got out, anywhere, just out, away from it all, then all I ever wanted to do was get back and start writing. Crazy. In those days I had a recurrent night-

must be stripped off. Give him the choice and he preferred the beautiful silence. The peace of stripping. But if they came he accepted them. They did him no harm.

He flicked another skin into the metal wastepaper basket and bit into another banana. When it was gone he would feel in the corners, between the molars, with his tongue, and sigh with contentment. How many doctors, wise men, had told him to pack it in, to have a change of diet and start a new life? But then how many doctors had told him he was too fat, needed to take more exercise, had bad teeth, incipient arthritis, a weak heart, bad circulation, bronchitis, pneumonia, traces of malarial fever, smallpox? He was a man, a mound of flesh, heir to all that flesh is heir to. Mobius sighed and rubbed the folds of his

---

mare. I was in my shorts, playing rugger in the mud against the giants. Proust, languid and bemonocled, kept guard behind the pack; Joyce, small and fiery, his moustache in perfect trim, darted through their legs, whisking out the ball and sending it flying to the wings: Dostoevsky, manic and bearded; Swift, ferocious and unstoppable; Chaucer, going like a terrier. And the pack, the pack itself, Tolstoy and Hugo and Homer and Goethe, Lawrence and Pascal and Milton and Descartes. Bearing down on me. Huge. Powerful. Totally confident. The ball kept coming out at me on the wing. It was a parcel of nappies neatly wrapped in plastic, 'We Clean Dirt' in violet lettering across it. I always seemed to be out there by myself, there was never anyone else on my side, but the ball would keep coming out of the loose at me. It always began like that, with the ball flying through the grey air towards my outstretched arms and then the pack bearing down, boots pounding the turf

stomach happily. It was a miracle he had survived this long when you thought of all the things that could have happened to him. And if so long then why not longer? – Time, he would say, she mean nothing to me. You see this? This fat? My body, she my clock. When I die she stop. And after all he had no need of clocks, there was a church on the other side of the street and it sounded for him, especially for him, a particular peal, at four o'clock. Then he would get up and make the bed (– You got to have order. Disorder in the little thing and that's the beginning of the end), wash his teeth and get his things together. No one had ever known him to get to the club after five (– You need time to meditate if you do a show like mine. Is like yoga, all meditation).

---

as in desperation I swung further and further out, knowing all the time I would never be able to make it to the line or have the nerve to steady and kick ahead. There was just me and this ball that was a parcel of nappies and all of them coming at me. Descartes in particular obsessed me. I would wake up sweating and wondering how it was possible to be so sure and yet so wrong. And why did they all have to keep coming for me like that, with Proust always drifting nonchalantly behind them, hair gleaming, boots polished, never in any hurry but always blocking my path? And what harm had I done any of them except read them? And now I wanted to forget them. Couldn't I be allowed to do that in peace? You don't think of it when you look at a tempting spine in a library or bookshop, but once you touch it you've had it. You're involved. It's worse than a woman. It's there in your body till the day you die and the harder you try and forget it the clearer it gets.

When Tony the manager took his annual holiday in the Bermudas he locked up the place and carried the keys away with him. Mobius, a stickler for routine and with a metaphysical need to satisfy, still got up at four, made his bed, emptied the banana skins into the communal dustbin in the back yard, cleaned his teeth, packed his things, and went on down to the club. He rattled the door and even tried to push it open with his shoulder, but it wouldn't give and he wasn't one to be put off by a thing like that. — I got my rights, same as you, he said to the policeman who took him in. Nobody's going to shut a door in my face and get away with it.

— That's no reason to break it down, the policeman said, staring in wonder at Mobius.

---

I tried aphorisms:

If a typewriter could read what it had written it would sue God.

He is another.

The trouble with the biological clock is it has no alarm.

No good. They weren't even good enough to fit end to end and send in as a poem to the *TLS*. In the streets Rilke walked beside me and whispered in my ear. He said beautiful things but I preferred whatever nonsense I might have thought up for myself if he hadn't been there. In the mornings I drove my cream van through the suburbs of West London and that kept me sane. I screamed to a halt, leapt out with my neat parcel of clean nappies, swapped it for the dirty ones waiting for me on the doorstep in the identical plastic wrapper, 'We Clean Dirt' in violet lettering. 'Like hell you do,' said a note pinned to the wrapper once. 'Take it back and try again.'

— I got my rights, Mobius said.

— You mean they don't pay you? the policeman asked.

— Sure they pay me, Mobius said.

— I mean in the holidays.

— Sure, Mobius said.

— Well then, the policeman said.

— I got my rights, Mobius said. He employ me, no?

— If it's a holiday why not go away somewhere? the policeman said. Give yourself a break.

— I doan want a break, Mobius said, I want my rights.

— I don't know about that, the policeman said. You've committed an offence against the law. I'm afraid I'll have to book you for it.

---

I took it back. They weren't my babies or my nappies and I didn't give a damn but my life was sliding off the rails and I didn't know what in God's name to do about it.

— Why don't you come and see Mobius the Stripper? Jenny said. It'll change your ideas. Give it a break and you'll all of a sudden see the light. That's fine, I said, except I've been saying just that for the last fifteen years and I'm still in the dark.

— That's because you don't trust, Jenny said. You've got no faith.

I had to admit she might be right. Unto those who have etcetera etcetera. But how does one contrive to have in the first place? There was a flaw somewhere but who was I to spot it?

— All right, Jenny said. Make an effort. Anybody can write something. Just put *something* down and then you'll feel better and you can come out with me.

Something. Mobius the Stripper was a genial man when in

— You doan understand, Mobius said to the policeman. This is my life. Just because he want to go to the fucking Bermudas doan mean I got to have my life ruined, eh?

— Are you American or something? the policeman asked, intrigued.

— You wanna see my British passport? Mobius said.

— Stay at home, the policeman advised him. Take it easy for a few days. We'll look into the matter when the manager returns.

The next time Tony took his holiday he gave Mobius the key of the club, but without the audience it wasn't the same, and after a day or two he just stayed in his room the whole time except for the occasional stroll down to the park and back, heavily protected by his big coat and Russian fur hat. But he

---

the bosom of his family. Etcetera. Etcetera etcetera. — Oh fuck off, I said I told you I didn't want to be disturbed.

— It'll do you good, she said, standing her ground. The worse the language I used the more she responded. She had a lot of background to make up for. — Besides, she said, it's all good experience.

— I don't need experience, I said. I need peace and quiet. And, if I'm lucky, a bit of inspiration.

— He'd give you that, Jenny said. Just to look at him is to feel inspired.

— What do you mean just to look at him? I said. What else are we expected to do?

— Go to hell, Jenny said.

— Tomorrow, I said.

— You said that yesterday.

— Nevertheless, I said. Tomorrow.

wasn't used to the streets, especially in the early evening when the tubes disgorged their contents, and it did him no good, no good at all. Inside the room he felt happier, but the break in the routine stopped him going to sleep and he spent the night with the light switched on. The bulb swung in the breeze and the voices dissolved him into a hundred parts. I first saw Mobius at a club in Buda. In Rio. In Albuquerque. A fine guy, Mobius. Is he? Oh yes, a fine guy. I remember going to see him and. I first heard of Mobius the Stripper from a kid down on the front in Marseilles. From a girl in Vienna. She was over there on a scholarship to study the cello and she. I met her in a restaurant. In a bar. She was blonde. Dark. A sort of dark skin. Long fingers. A cellist's fingers. There's nobody like Mobius, she said.

---

Jenny began to sob. It was impressive. I was impressed. — Just because I have big feet, she said, you think you can push me around like that. — Jenny, I said. Please. I like big feet.

— You don't, she sobbed. You find them ridiculous. When she sobbed she really sobbed. Nothing could stem the tide.

— In men, I said. I find them ridiculous in men. In women I find them a sign of solidity. Stability.

— You're just laughing at me, she said. You despise me because of my big feet.

M.E. The foot fetishist. He was a quiet man, scholarly and abstemious. Everyone who ever met him said he was almost a saint. Not quite but almost. Yet deep inside there throbbed etcetera etcetera.

— But I don't, I said. You've no idea what I feel about feet. I can't have enough of them. That's just what I like about you, Jenny. Your big feet.

Mobius smiled and listened to the voices. They came and went inside his head and if that's where they liked to be he had no objection. There was room and more. But he missed his sleep and he knew bronzed Tony had a point when he said: – Mobius, you look a sight.

That was the day the club reopened. – Why don't you take a holiday same as everyone? Tony said. You must have a tidy bit stacked away by now.

– A holiday from what? Mobius asked him.

– I don't know, Tony said. Mobius upset him, he didn't know which way to take him. Maybe one of these days he'd cease to pull them in and then he could get rid of him, – Just a holiday, he said. From work.

---

She stopped crying. Just like that. – You're despicable, she said. You're obscene.

– Look, Jenny, I said. I'll come with you. I'd love to see this chap. But tomorrow. OK?

An incredible girl, Jenny. A great tactician. – You promise? she said, before I had time to draw breath.

– You know I'd love to go, I said. I just don't want to be a drag on you. And if I'm sitting there thinking of my work all the time instead of being convivial and all I –

– You'll see, Jenny said. You'll love him. He's a lovely man.

Lovely or not I didn't think I could face them, either Jenny or her stripper, so I locked the door and went out into the park. Walking around there and kicking my feet in the leaves and seeing all those nannies and things kept the rest of it at bay. Had Rilke seen this nanny? Or Proust that child? Had Hopkins seen this tree, this leaf? So what did they have to teach me? They

— Look, Mobius said to him. That the difference between
us, Tony. You work and you spit on your work. But for me my
work is my life.

— OK, Tony said. I'm not complaining.

— Is there a holiday from life? Mobius asked him. Answer
me that, Tony.

— For God's sake! Tony said. Can't you talk straight ever?
You're not on stage now, you know.

— You just answer me first, Mobius said. Is there a holiday
from life, Tony?

— I don't know what you're talking about, Tony said, and
when Mobius began to laugh, his great belly heaving, he added
under his breath: You shit.

---

were talking about something else altogether. They were just
about as much use to me as I was to them. And if it's eternity
they wanted, why pick on me? There are plenty of other fools
around for them to try their vampire tricks on. I can do without
them, thank you very much. And if it's this tree I want to see
they only get in the way. And if it isn't what use am I to myself?
Their trees they've already seen.

After a while, though, I felt the urge to get back in there
and sit down in front of that blasted sheet of white paper. What
use is this tree even if I do see it? No use to me or to the world.
And even if it is, who says I *can* see it? When I sit down in front
of that sheet of paper I have this feeling I want to tear right in
and get everything down. Everything. And then what happens?
He was a small man with a. I remember once asking Charles
and. Gerald looked round. Christopher turned. When Jill saw.
When Robert saw. Elizabeth Nutely was. Geraldine Bluett was.

At home he said to his wife: — That guy Mobius. He's a nut.

— Is he still drawing them in? his wife asked as she passed him the toast.

— I don't know what they see in him, Tony said. A fat bloody foreigner stripping in public. Downright obscene it is. And they roll in to see him. It makes you despair of the British public.

— Try the blackcurrant, his wife said. And then: — You hired him. You couldn't go on enough about him at first.

— It makes you sick, Tony said. He pulled the jam towards him. Bloody perverted they are, he said. Bloody twisted.

But when Mobius said it wasn't sexual it was metaphysical he had a point. Take off the layers and get down to the basics. One day the flesh would go and then the really basic would

---

Hilary McPherson wasn't exactly the. Everything is the enemy of something, and when my pen touches the paper I go blank. Stories. Stories and stories. Mobius the Stripper sat in his penthouse flat and filed his nails. Sat in his bare room and picked his nose. Stories and stories. Anyone can write them. All you need is a hide thick enough to save you from boring yourself sick. Jack turned suddenly and said. Count Frederick Prokovsky, a veteran of the Crimea. Horst Voss, the rowing coach. Peter Bender, overseer of a rubber plantation in. Etcetera etcetera. This one and this one and this one. When all the time it's crying out in me (Henry James was much obsessed by this but there the similarity between us ends. Goodbye, Henry James, goodbye, Virginia Woolf, goodbye, goodbye) crying out in me to *say everything, everything.*

They keep peacocks in the park. I don't know why. But they do. One of them was strutting about in the path in front of me.

come to light. Mobius waited patiently for that day.

— You read Prust, he would say. Nitch. Jennet. Those boys.
See what they say. All the same. They know the truth. Is all a
matter of stripping.

— You talk too much, Moby, the girls said to him. You're
driving us crazy with all your talk.

— You gotta talk when you strip, Mobius explained to them.
You gotta get the audience involved.

— You can have music, the girls said. Music's nice. Whoever
heard of a stripper talking?

— OK, Mobius admitted. Perhaps I do like to talk. Like that
I talk I feel my essential self emerging. Filling the room.

Outside the club, though, Mobius rarely opened his mouth.

---

With big feet like Jenny. Who was I to say if big feet are attrac-
tive or not? And why ask me anyway? Think of the stripper
Mobius with his nightly ritual, slowly getting down to the primal
scene and after that what? Why do men do things like that and
do they even know themselves, etcetera etcetera? All the stories
in the world but you've only got one body and who would ever
exchange the former for the latter except every single second-
rate writer who's ever lived? And they still live. Proliferate. And
believe in themselves, what's more. Why then the daily anguish
and the certainty that if I could only start the pen moving over
the sheet of paper my life would alter, alter, as they say, beyond
the bounds of recognition? Because I've read them all? The van
Gogh letters and the life of Rimbaud and the Hopkins
Notebooks and the N. of M.L.B. Have they conned me even
into this? It was possible. Everything is possible. — Tell me the
truth, I said to the peacock with the big feet. Go on, you bastard.

Certainly he never spoke to himself, and as for the voices, if they wanted to settle for a while inside his head, who was he to order them away? He sat on the bed and stared at the wall, eating bananas and dozing. I first saw. I first heard. I remember His Excellency telling me about Mobius the Stripper. In Prague it was, that wonderful city. I was acting as private secretary to the Duke and had time on my hands, I was down and out in Paris and London. A girl called Bertha Pappenheim first mentioned Mobius to me. Not the famous Bertha Pappenheim, another.

Once or twice he would pull a chair up to the mirror on the dressing-table, which stood inevitably in the bay window, and stare and stare into his own grey eyes. Then he would push the chair violently back and go over to the bed again. — For what

---

Tell me the truth or fuck off. A woman with an unpleasant little runt of a white poodle backed away down an alley. — Don't you want the truth? I asked her. She turned and beetled off towards the gates. — Lady! I shouted after her. Don't you want the truth?

It's always the same. That's what gets me down. If I can say *anything* then why say anything. And yet everything's there to be said. Round and round. Mobius sat on his bed and ate one banana after another. But did he? Did he?

The bird had gone and I sat down on a bench and looked up at the sky through the trees. Jenny would have been and gone by now. Or perhaps not been at all. I sometimes wondered if Jenny knew quite as many people as she said she did. Wondered if perhaps there was only me she knew in the whole of London. Otherwise how to explain her persistence? Unless those feet of hers kept perpetually carrying her back over the ground they had once trodden. Myth. Ritual. An idea. More than an idea.

is life? he would say. Chance. And what is *my* life? The result of a million and one chances. But behind chance is truth. The whole problem is to get behind chance to the TRUTH! That was when the jockstrap came off and it brought the house down. But Mobius hadn't finished with them. Sitting cross-legged on the little wooden stage, staring at more than his navel, he let them have the facts of life, straight from the chest.

— Beyond a man's chance is his necessity. But how many find? I ask you. You think this is a seshual thing, but for why you come to see me? Because I give you the truth. Is a metaphysical something, is the truth. Is the necessity behind the chance. For each man is only one truth and so many in the world as each man is truths.

---

A metaphor for life. — It is! I shouted, suddenly understanding. It is! It is! A metaphor for life!

A little group of people was standing on the path under the trees. One or two park wardens. A fat man with one of those Russian fur hats. My friend the poodle woman. I waved to them. They seemed to expect it. One of the wardens stepped forward and asked politely why I was chasing the peacocks and using bad language. The man was preposterous. Couldn't he see me sitting silent on the bench? I'd chased Pascal down a back alley once, but the peacocks? What am I to peacocks or they to me? I said to the man.

— I saw you, the poodle woman said. Chasin and abusin.

— Don't be more absurd than you can help, I said to her.

— Don't you dare to talk to me like that, young man, she said. What would Descartes have done in my place?

— Chasin peacocks and usin abusin language, she said.

Mobius, staring into his own grey eyes in the little room in Notting Hill, occasionally sighed, and his gaze would wander over the expanse of flesh exposed and exposable. Sometimes his right hand would hover over the drawer of his dressing-table, where certain private possessions were kept but would as quickly move away again. That was too easy. Yet if you talk of necessity how many versions are there? His hand hovered but the drawer remained unopened.

— These girls, he would say, they excite you seshually. But once you seen me your whole life is change. He had a way of riding the laughter, silencing it. For why? For you learn from me the difference between on one hand clockwork and on other hand necessity. Clockwork is clockwork. One. Two. In. Out.

---

— Are you going to stand there and listen to this woman's grotesque accusations? I asked them.

— It is an offence under the regulations, the warden said, to chase the peacocks.

— But I love those birds, I said. I love their big feet. For some reason I was still sitting there on that bench and they were standing grouped together under the trees staring in my direction. What would I want to go chasing them for? I said.

How could they be expected to understand? Or, understanding, to believe? Had I a beard like Tolstoy's? A moustache like Rilke's? — Gentlemen, I said. I apologise. Good evening.

— He's goin away, the woman said. You can't let him go away like that. He insulted and abused me.

— In that case, madam, the warden said, I suggest you consult a lawyer. Bless his silver tongue. The first thing I'm going to do when success comes my way is give a donation to

But Necessity she a goddess. She turn your muscles to water and your bones to oil. One day you meet her and you will see that Mobius is right.

He went home after that session more slowly than usual. If he was giving them the truth where was the truth? His heart heavy with the weight of years he opened the drawer and took out his little friend. Cupping it in his hand he felt its weight. There was no hesitation in his movements now and why should there be? If his life had a logic then this was it. The weight on his heart pressed him to this point. When you have stripped away everything the answer will be there, but if so, why wait? Easy to say it's too easy but why easier than waiting? As always,

---

the wardens of the London parks.

I was shaken, though. And who wouldn't be? Examples of prejudice are always upsetting. Upsetting but exhilarating too. They make you want to fight back. Something had happened down there inside me in those few minutes and now I couldn't wait to get back. This was it. After all those years.

There was no message from Jenny on the door. Not even a single word like 'Bastard!' or 'Fuck you!' or any of the other affectionate little expressions we use when we are sufficiently intimate with a person. Well fuck her. I could do without her. Without them all. I was sitting at my desk with this white sheet of paper in front of me and suddenly it was easy. I bent over it, pen poised, wrist relaxed, the classic posture. It was all suddenly so easy I couldn't understand what had kept me back for so long.

I looked at the white page. At the pen. At my wrist. I began to laugh. You have to laugh at moments like that. It's the only thing to do. When I had finished laughing I got up and went

he did everything methodically. When he had found the right spot on his temple he straightened a little and waited for the steel to gather a little warmth from the flesh. – So I come to myself at last, Mobius said. To the centre of myself. And he said: – Is my necessity and my truth. And is example to all. He stared into his own grey eyes and felt the coldness of the metal, his finger tightened on the trigger and the voices were there again. Cocking his head on one side and smiling, Mobius listened to what they had to say. He had time on his hands and to spare. Resting the barrel against his brow and smiling to himself in the mirror as the bulb swung in the breeze over his head, Mobius waited for them to finish.

---

to the window. What I couldn't work out was if I had actually believed it or really known all along that today was going to be different from any other day. That between everything and something would once again fall the shadow. Leaving me with nothing. Nothing.

I turned round and sat down at the desk again. At least if Jenny had been there it wouldn't have been so bad. We could have talked. I looked at my watch. There was still time. She might still come.

I picked up the pen and wrote my name across the top of the sheet, for no reason that I could fathom. And then, suddenly, out of the blue, it started to come. Perhaps it was only one story, arbitrary, incomplete, but suddenly I knew that it would make its own necessity and in the process give me back my lost self. Dear Jenny. Dear Mobius. Dear Peacock. 'Gone out. Do not disturb.' I scrawled on a sheet of paper, pinned it to the door and locked it. Then I sat down and began to write.

# The Bird Cage

So you are in the house at last. How well you describe the room. The sea. The window. The bird in the cage. The mirror. And then in the mirror the cage, the window and the sea.

When I read what you say I long to be there, with you, in that room brimming with light and the sea and the bird.

You ask me to come. You describe the way the light fills the room. You describe the way the mirror reflects the light which bounces off the sea. You describe the way the song of the bird mingles with the sound of the waves.

\* \* \* \* \*

I will catch the train this afternoon. In a few hours I will be there. Tomorrow morning I will wake and see the foot of the bed in the mirror and then the cage and the bird and the window and the sea. Last night I dreamed about the bird. About the yellowness of its plumage. You tell me about his song, the sound of his voice, and in my dream it is translated into colours, into the colour of his plumage. I wish I knew what that meant. What that dream meant, the transposition in the dream.

\* \* \* \* \*

I am here now and you are gone. I came and we were together and now you are gone.

I am glad you are not here. I am glad to be able to possess the room and myself as you possessed it before I came. I am glad to be able to stand at the window and look into the sea and let the song of the bird fill me up entirely. I am glad to wake alone and look in the mirror and see the foot of the bed and the bird in his cage and the window and the sea outside. I am glad to be able to take possession of it as you took possession of it. In that way I feel I am getting to know you as well as I know myself.

I am glad you have had to go away. I am glad to be alone here with nothing but the sea and the gulls and the bird in the cage. I stand for hours under his cage, looking at the sea. The light reflecting off the sea almost hurts. It makes everything in the room seem to splinter into a thousand fragments, as if it could not contain itself, there was so much light. I never draw the curtains. At night I feel myself going to sleep in the middle of the sea. When I wake in the morning I keep my eyes closed for a moment, feeling the light exploding in my body. I don't count the days. Sometimes I imagine I have not yet arrived and only have your descriptions to fire my imagination. Sometimes it is almost too much to bear in the present.

I am glad to be here by myself but I begin to miss you. I wonder why you have not yet returned, what it is that is keeping you so long. I have begun to think of how you looked those last few days. I have begun to wonder if you are ever coming back. Yesterday I walked to the farm with the intention of ringing you, but when I got there I couldn't do it. Won't you write to me? Won't you tell me when you are coming back?

\* \* \* \* \*

This morning I walked to the farm and asked to use the phone. I dialled your number but when I heard the phone ringing in your flat I put the instrument straight back. I think I couldn't face hearing the sound of you withdrawing when you learned who it was at the other end. Perhaps tomorrow I will have more courage, be able to go through with it.

\* \* \* \* \*

I have decided to go away. I have decided that you will not come back here till I go away. I stand at the window and look at the sea and I know that I will have to go away. I will bring the bird round to the farm when I bring them the key. Perhaps when you learn that I have gone away you will be able to return.

I had expected an explanation but you have provided none. I had expected the phone to ring in my flat but it was silent. And now you write as though nothing had happened. You write about the bird and the room as you did before. Before I came. As if I had never been and you had never gone and left me there, for a day or two you said, while you dealt with urgent matters in town. What is the meaning of your letter?

\* \* \* \* \*

You write and ask me to come, as though nothing had happened. I do not know what to make of what you write. You say you are selling the house and want me to see it for one last time. I cannot understand what it is you are asking.

\* \* \* \* \*

You beg me to answer and let you know if I have received your
letters. You tell me the house is sold with the bird and the bed
and the mirror and everything else. You say you want to see me
and beg me to answer. How can I answer a letter like that?

* * * * *

You write and tell me the owner has allowed the house to go
to ruin. You write go to ruin as if that were the most natural
thing in the world, and as if the English were correct. Perhaps
it is but it feels wrong to me. I would have said fall into ruin,
but perhaps it is I who am at fault. You write that you have
been back and walked along the beach and pushed open the
door because no one lives in the house any more and it is an
adventure to walk along the beach and see this lovely and
deserted house right up against the sea which is not locked, and
climb the stairs which are rotting and enter the bedroom. You
write that you would like to buy back the house and restore it.
You write that the mirror still stands in the bedroom, reflecting
the foot of the bed and the window and the sea. You write that
the cage is still there but the bird has gone. I don't know why
you write these things to me or what you want of me. You say
you do not know if the bird is dead or the owner has found him
a better cage. I don't know why you write like this. I remember
the light in the room when we woke in the morning and the
light of the evening when I stood by myself at the window, but
most of all I remember how I imagined the room when you first
wrote to me about it.

* * * * *

How can I answer your letters? What do you want me to say? I showed my little girl the picture you had drawn, of the mirror and the room reflected in it, and, beyond the window, the sea. She said the bird was singing. I asked her how she knew but she giggled the way children do and wouldn't answer.

I don't think you understand. I don't think you have much idea of what happens to us in our lives. I don't think you see that we are all in cages, but the cages are our lives. You wanted to build a cage around yourself and then you were afraid when you saw the bars. But there is no need to build. The cages are our lives. When we recognise this we can sing. That is what I think at least.

*  *  *  *  *

I say these words to myself: the sea, the window, the bird, the cage, the room, the mirror, and then the room again, the cage, the window and the sea. They are like the bars of my cage. My little girl asks me if I will ever take her to the room in the house by the sea. I tell her: You are there. You are in the room. There is no need to go. She does not hear when I speak. She looks at the picture. The picture on the page. I say: Turn the page. Let us look at another picture. She does not hear. She is absorbed by what is in front of her, as children are. Turn the page, I say. Turn the page and let us look at another picture. But she does not hear.

# Waiting

Martha, a widow, kissed her son first on the forehead and then on either cheek, both eyes, the nose, the chin, the ears and the mouth. She held him for a moment, then pushed him away from her. He turned, creaking a little in his new army boots, and left the house without looking back.

After that, each morning, before she got out of bed, and each night, before turning over on her side – the position in which she found it easiest to sleep – she said aloud to herself: forehead, cheeks, eyes, nose, chin, ears, mouth. Sometimes she added: shoulders, back, chest, stomach, arms, legs, hands, feet, shoulders, back, chest, stomach, arms, legs, hands, feet; shoulders, back, chest, stomach, arms, legs, hands, feet.

Letters arrived from the Front. She turned them over this way and that, then let them lie on the table. She repeated her litany, then tore open the envelope, pulled out the sheets, peered short-sightedly at the handwriting, hunting for the signature, then pushed them roughly back into the envelope. When she laid the table for the evening meal she would brush the envelope into a corner and then, when it floated to the floor, grab it violently so that the letter inside crumpled even further, and stuff it into a drawer as if it had caused her some offence.

She frequently sat at the table in the kitchen and counted aloud the contents of the drawers: knives, forks, spoons, breadknife, carving knife, ladle, saucepans, frying pan, kettle. She lay in bed staring up at the ceiling and kissed her son again, holding him in her arms and then pushing him abruptly away: forehead, cheeks, eyes, nose, chin, ears, mouth; forehead, cheeks, eyes, nose, chin, ears, mouth. Then she turned over on her side and went to sleep.

In the street, walking to the shops, she went over the contents of the linen cupboard in her mind: sheets, pillowcases, blankets, towels; sheets, pillowcases, blankets, towels.

Letters were infrequent. When they arrived it was many weeks after they had been written. She sat in her customary chair in the kitchen and looked at the envelope: forehead, cheeks, eyes, nose, chin, ears, mouth; forehead, cheeks, eyes, nose, chin, ears, mouth. Then she tore it open, scanned the writing, searching for the signature, and thrust it away from her: forehead, cheeks, eyes, nose, chin, ears, mouth; shoulders, back, chest, stomach, arms, legs, hands, feet.

She did not try to follow the course of the war from the newspapers or to listen to what people said in the streets. When it was over it would be over. Meanwhile, time had to be used up.

She laid out the crockery on the kitchen table but did not look at it as she went over it in her mind: cups, saucers, plates, bowls, glasses. And the cutlery: knives, forks, spoons, breadknife, carving knife, ladle.

She slept little, waking in the middle of the night and finding herself staring at a corner of the room with unseeing eyes. Then she would turn over on her back and go over it all again: forehead, cheeks, eyes, nose, chin, ears, mouth. After that, sometimes, she found it possible to sleep again.

One day the ladle was missing. She pulled out all the drawers, knelt and peered into the backs of all the cupboards. It will turn up, she thought, it's there, somewhere, I shouldn't have taken it out all the time to look at it, I should give up all this counting, memorising. I shouldn't be so anxious.

But it didn't turn up. She tried not to think about it. She stopped herself reciting the contents of the kitchen drawers. Yet she went on opening cupboards, feeling in the recesses with her rough hands.

After that she had a dream. God spoke to her in her dream. His words were comforting but she had a sense of anguish, hearing him, mingled with a feeling of overwhelming relief. He towered over her bed, distinctly visible in all His aspects, a big man with a strong face and beard and a small scar on the left side of his chin. His words poured over her like oil, continuous, indistinguishable, yet perfectly clear in meaning. She stared up at Him in wonder, noting His white hair, powerful nose, regal body in its white robe – or perhaps it was light, a body made of light, not a robe at all. She was suddenly unsure, sat up to look more closely, then noticed that one of His arms was missing.

The shock was physical: a blow to the heart. She struggled to understand what it was that confronted her and saw now that all one side of Him was dark, a vacuum. She wanted to protest, to say, but You are God, no part of You can be missing, You must be all there, is this a joke or something? – only it was as if there was no longer any need for that, she knew now beyond all doubt, and though His voice continued to roll over her in its soothing flow, she had ceased to listen, ceased, finally, to see.

# Fuga

One day he took me round to see his mother and sister they worked as seamstresses I don't know the area exactly in the northern suburbs somewhere there are so many alleys and back streets but the flat itself was clean there was cloth all over the place and the wallpaper crying out it seemed like a continuation of the material of the dresses the mother sat at a large table in the middle of the room he introduced us the sister had got up she was close to the wall I could feel she was frightened she brought us something to drink just for the two of us the mother didn't take anything and she didn't either something sweet rather syrupy but she wouldn't sit down nervously hugging the wall or fetching things he asked me afterwards how I liked her I sensed he wanted us to be friends maybe something more you could drop in when you're passing they'll always be glad to see you they're always at home he didn't say much to them didn't exchange many words the mother sat at the table in the middle and got on with the sewing the cutting I knew he lived at home but he didn't seem to spend much time there it was as if he was visiting them formally once a week that sort of thing the sister was cowering against the wall in her flowery dress against the flowery paper it was as if she was trying to disappear altogether she's shy she likes you he said afterwards she warmed to you did you notice how she sat and watched while you drank he wanted us to be friends and I liked her I felt drawn to her as I did to him though she was as silent as he was garrulous just drop in he said she is always there she will be pleased to give you a drink he even drew me a map with a cross for the bus stop and another for the building that was how it started I found my way back I found my way there at first I liked sitting here with the material all round and the two of them working away I tried to talk to her and she answered she always answered and so precisely but she never started a conversation herself I liked to sit there they seemed calmer when he wasn't there sipping the syrup I don't know what it was she would get up when I came and return with it and put it on the table and I would sit and sip and close my eyes and hear their scissors the mother never got up it was the sister who let me in let me out got up and fetched the syrup or answered the door but always pressed against the wall when she moved at first I found it pleasant just to sit there and talk so little and hear the sound of the scissors but after a while I wanted to see her in different surroundings a different atmosphere I asked her to come out with me but she wouldn't she wanted to but she wouldn't I looked at the mother and she went on sewing and snipping I asked her why not but she just shook her head for a stroll I said or a drink or perhaps they would both come out but the mother didn't answer and she shook her head and wouldn't look at me her hands rubbing rubbing behind her back twined together I asked him why she wouldn't come out he urged me to press her again confirmed that she really wanted to but didn't quite know how to accept and then all of a sudden it came to me that outside she would be nothing that she only existed against that wallpaper in that room with the mother sewing and the two of them busy that there would be nothing to say I tried once more but without much conviction I don't know why he comes now every day why he brought him in the first place I had so much wanted him to bring someone to bring a friend anyone to see someone who wasn't him and wasn't her I liked the way he sat upright hesitant never taking anything for granted I wanted to talk to him but I had nothing to say he asked me out finally he asked me out I wanted to go but I had grown rigid she went on sewing I wanted to go I wanted him to take my hand and lead me but I couldn't go my body had turned to stone what would I do outside I know here it is quiet it is peaceful I have something to do what use is walking up and down in the street or even holding hands there was so much of me that wanted to go but something held me my body was stone I knew then that I could never go though I wanted it so much I wanted even more to stay here to look after her to sew for him and for her there was something that was stronger than every desire that held me that pressed me as if I had no other territory than this as if there would be no air in another place and so I shook my head and at first he pressed me and I hoped he would take my hand take the decision away from me but then finally I saw that he too had accepted it and so it was mother sits there she has sheltered us she has fed us they sit there sewing the two of them I can see her turning into the wallpaper flattening herself more and more against the walls of the room until she disappears altogether I brought him round he was the only one the others wouldn't have had the patience I felt he was the only one when I first met him I told him about them I brought him round I left him there at first I had high hopes he came back regularly something

seemed to be happening she was relaxing she was moving away
from the walls mother sat in the centre smiling getting on with
her work I think she too hoped we all hoped she came forward
she even sat at the table with him watched him drink it seemed
to be progressing smoothly inevitably and then all at once it was
finished it was smashed as if in the end she could not do it
though I willed her to and mother willed her to but this was
her element this was the air in which she could breathe it was
like a death for me it was like my death my own feeling that I
too was locked here and perhaps it was for the best no one
screamed it was all so quiet and yet it was the end of something
the end of a hope but perhaps that is life the end of all hopes
that is when real life begins the acceptance of life the life we
have I stay out days at a time nights at a time and when I come
home she gets up and brings the glass and the sweet liquid I
don't ask anyone back any more there are just the three of us
the scissors snip away I watch them sometimes I draw them as
they work their heads bent or I paint the wallpaper the chimney
one day I will paint her at the moment when she realised she
belonged to the room the moment when the wallpaper claimed
her it won't be about her it will be about me it won't even be
about me it will be about mother silent and serious in the centre
or about something else something only we can feel that is
perhaps what I will do while they work to pay the rent to keep
us here where we have always been where we will always be for
ever and ever just the three of us and the wallpaper and the
sound of the scissors and the silence.

# Memories of a Mirrored Room in Hamburg

— There was no war, he says. There were no trenches. There was no mud.

Six times mirrored in the room: a round, glass-topped table; a vase with a single lily; a bottle; two glasses; a chair; a man in uniform without his cap; a naked woman on his knee.

He says: — There was no war. There was no mud. I did not die.

In the mirrored walls, the mirrored floor, the mirrored ceiling: a vase; a bottle; a chair; a man in uniform with a naked woman on his knee.

— Prosit! she says, and raises her glass.

— There was no mud, he says. There was no gas. I did not die. I am not dead.

— To the future! she says, and drinks.

He laughs.

Her arms round his neck. Six times mirrored.

— Tell, she says. Tell me more. Tell me a little more.

— There was no, he says. I did not.

The opening. The opening of her body. In the floor. The ceiling.

– Tell, she says. Tell me. Her arm round his neck. Tell. Her hand on his flies.

His head thrown back. Her hand.

Her arms round my

Sagging body on my

The table. The two glasses. The bottle. The vase. The flower.

Her hands at his back, caressing.

– Tell, she says, Tell about the

He says: – There was no gas. There were no shells. I did not die.

Flesh on my

How did I

– Prosit! she says. They drink, heads thrown back. Reflected are: the table, the vase, the flower, the bottle, the man, the woman, heads thrown back, drinking.

– Now, he says.

– No, she says.

– Now, he says.

– No, she says. Tell me more. Tell me more.

Kiss. They kiss. – Tell me more, she says. In his mouth, she says. To the future.

The opening. The opening of her body reflected in the floor. The floor in the ceiling. – Tell, she says. Her hand on his flies.

His head thrown back. Her hand on his flies.

– There was no war, he says. I did not.

The table. The bottle. The two glasses. The vase. The flower. The man in his uniform. The naked, sagging woman.

– Now, he says.

– No, she says. Not yet.

— Now, he says. Now.

She raises her glass. Tosses her red hair. — Again the future! He laughs. She says: — Tell. Tell me you must tell.

— Now, he says. Now. It must.

— No, she says, mouth on his. Tell about the. Tell about the. Tell about the mud.

— There was no mud, he says. There was no war. There was no gas.

The room. Six times reflected are: the table, the vase, the flower, the bottle, the two glasses, the chair, the man, the woman. Nothing else in the mirrored room.

He says: — There was no mud. There were no trenches. I am not dead.

Her arms round my

Flesh on my

Raise her glass and

Round my neck her lips on

— Tell, she says. Tell me more. Her hand in. Head back. Mouth open.

— Tell me, she says.

— There was no.

— No what?

— There was no.

— No?

— Now, he says. It must.

— No, she says. Not yet, she says.

— Yes, he says. Now.

— Tell, she says. Tell about the.

— I am not. I was not.

On the floor savagely I

Arms round my face back in my

– Prosit! she says, and tips back the glass.

On the floor and her above lapping up and lapping up how did I come where is it where is it now I come I

– The future! she says, and raises her glass. Seven times raises her glass in the empty room.

On the floor and where I

Seven times her arms round his neck vase on the table her sagging weight on his knee they kiss they kiss.

Coming now rolling on the glass the floor the glass she laughs head back mouth open how did I come here where is the exit where is the where.

Laughs, holding out her glass, tossing her hair, he refills, she says: – Tell. Tell.

– I did not. there was no.

Where is the exit where

Raises her glass and toasts the future the end of the end of the end of the

Coming now rolling glass floor cold smooth reflect the rolling over and over where are you now where are you now where

– I was not there. I did not fight. I did not.

– I, she says, rolling. I fight. I, rolling, over and over now on top now below, I, she says, I fight, she says, I fight for I fight for I fight for I

The table. The vase. The flower. The bottle. The two glasses. The chair. The man in uniform. The naked red-haired woman on his knee.

– Warm me, she says. Warm me warm me warm me warm me warm me.

Faster rolling faster into the table the vase crashing bottle breaking her back red with blood I

— Prosit! she says, tips back her glass, red hair tossing.

I drink I lick I come I

— Now! she says. Yes now! she says.

There was no mud. I did not. I am not.

— Yes now! she says, yes now yes now yes now yes now yes now yes.

Rolling and rolling now he says now he says quick he says I he says now he says now

The table. the chair. The vase. The flower. The bottle. The man in uniform. The naked sagging woman on his knee. They raise their glasses.

He says: — There was no war. There were no trenches. There was no mud. I did not die.

The mirrored room. In the ceiling, the floor, the four walls: a table, a vase, a single lily, a bottle, two glasses, a chair, a man in uniform, without his cap, a naked woman on his knee.

— There was no war, he says. I did not die. I am not dead.

Did not. Am not.

Did not. Am not.

— Yes, he says. There was no war. There was no mud. I did not die. I am not. I am not dead.

# He

He heard on the telephone. His friend's mother rang him up one Saturday evening as he was preparing to take his bath and told him his friend was dead. The words went right into him, quite physically. He felt them entering his body, making no sense but leaving him with the certain knowledge that they would lodge there inside him, like stones, that in the coming days they would insist more and more on his paying attention to them, and that he would never be able to assimilate them entirely. As always on such occasions the mind holds on to the little immediate practical things: Was she alone? Was she all right? Did she want to come straight down and talk? No, she had a friend with her. The police had just been and gone. They had told her that her son had been found dead in his room by his landlady. They would not say if it had been an accident or if he had deliberately taken his own life. She did not sound particularly anguished, she said herself that she had not yet really taken in the news, that that would take time, that she merely wanted him as her son's closest friend to know at once.

When he was eventually able to put down the receiver he found himself face to face with those first words: 'Alan is dead.'

He knew he would not be able to digest them. He did not try.
He phoned the dead man's other close friends and told them:
'This is going to come as a shock to you. I'm sorry. Alan is dead.'
He phoned the woman who was at the time closest to his friend
and told her. He was not prepared for her scream or her words:
'But I'm so full of him.' No one else that evening had spoken
so directly.

He went to bed and, because he was at the time on antibi-
otics for some minor infection and the drug exhausted him, he
went straight to sleep. He woke many times in the night and
each time it seemed to him that he had not been asleep at all,
but each time he promptly fell asleep again. He had many
dreams, some of them so vivid that they seemed to be only the
continuation of the events of that day. He dreamed that he
arrived at the hospital where his friend had been taken and was
shown the corpse. He bent over and listened to the heart: it was
still beating. He called a nurse: 'He's alive. He's not dead at all.'
The nurse called a doctor. Between them they revived the
patient. 'You were going to have him taken away and buried
and all the time he was alive and breathing,' he said to them
accusingly. 'If I hadn't come along who knows what might have
happened?' He was furious with the hospital, but there was a
huge unspoken area of relief: it had all been a mistake; his friend
was alive and well.

He woke from that dream convinced that his friend was
alive and at once remembered that he was dead. He fell asleep
again and was talking to another friend, a rabbi: 'You will say
Kaddish for him, won't you?' he said, and the rabbi nodded. He
woke, surprised at his knowledge of the word and once more
aware of his ignorance of matters of ritual, Christian or Jewish.
Did one say what he had said? Did it make sense? Do rabbis say

Kaddish in the same way as priests say prayers? He was surprised
to find that he, who had no faith and no instruction in any reli-
gion, should be so concerned with such matters at this moment.
Perhaps it was that his friend had a strong religious streak in
him, though he could hardly have been called devout. Or
perhaps it was that in moments like this we all reach out to the
impersonal forms of prayer and lamentation, whatever our
beliefs, feeling instinctively that they can carry the burden of
our sorrow in a way mere thought or dialogue cannot. The next
day he even wrote to another friend, a novitiate nun, asking her
to pray for the soul of his friend and for that of his mother.

But it was not a time for writing letters. It seemed to have
become a time for talking to the bewildered survivors. Every
death leaves behind it unanswered questions, but a sudden death
at the age of thirty leaves more than most. In addition, the facts
themselves were confused and only emerged in fragments, as the
police released another bit of information or the landlady
remembered another detail and passed it onto the mother who
relayed it to him. At first the weight of evidence seemed to be
in favour of an accidental death. He had been going to spend
the weekend with friends in Cromer, but on the Saturday afternoon the landlady heard the radio playing in his room. She
knocked but there was no reply. She tried the door but it was
locked. She called her husband, who broke down the door. They
found him lying on his bed, covered in vomit, an empty whisky
bottle and a full bottle of aspirin beside him. Though he was
not in the habit of drinking alone it was possible that he had
done so in a fit of depression and then gone to sleep and choked
on his vomit. Moreover, if he had intended to kill himself it
was likely that he would have left a note and none had been
found.

The next day, however, the information came through that there had in fact been a note, which the police had taken away. What the contents were they would not at the moment divulge. A post-mortem and inquest were being held and the truth would no doubt emerge in due time. The likelihood of suicide, however, was now strong. But if it was indeed suicide, why? Every one of his friends agreed that things had never been so good for him, that perhaps for the first time in his life there appeared to be a meaningful future ahead of him, that both his private and his professional life had taken a decided turn for the better in the past few months. Could anyone think of a less likely time for him to commit suicide? His friends came and they talked and talked. For all of them suicide could only be seen as a rejection of themselves and of all they might have meant to the dead man. They could not understand it and they could not bear to be alone with their perplexity. The sudden death brought them together in a way the dead man, in the course of his life, had never been able to do. The talk was endless.

It was not till four days later that the police released a photostat of the note. Yes, it was undoubtedly a suicide note, but it answered none of the questions. It merely said that as he did what he did he thought with affection of his mother, his landlady and his friends and that none of them had ever given him any cause for complaint. He listed his friends.

And yet, if this was the case, why had he done it? The post-mortem revealed that he had in fact taken enough aspirin to kill an elephant, washed down with whisky, on top of a meal carefully designed to keep everything down. There had clearly been nothing haphazard about the attempt. Always meticulous in his attention to detail, he had excelled himself here. First he had

made sure no one would call on him unexpectedly by saying
that he would be away for the weekend. Then he had phoned
his mother and asked her to send a telegram to his friends in
Cromer, saying that he was not going to be able to make it. A
little later he had phoned his mother again to reassure her that
he was fine, just didn't feel up to all that travel and would probably go for a walk that afternoon, she was not to worry, he
would see her at the concert on the Monday evening as planned.
He had then had his meal, bought the whisky, told his landlady
he was off, double-locked the door, written the note, and swallowed the tablets. If it had not been for the radio he would
certainly not have been found till the Monday night.

The talk continued. He found himself in the position of
prop and comforter to the baffled and the hysterical – having
them round, talking to them, calming them down, breaking the
news to others, keeping everyone up to date with the details of
the note, the post-mortem, the funeral arrangements. In a way
this was a relief. He did not have to be by himself too much,
did not have to face the alien thing inside his body: the voice
over the phone saying: 'Alan is dead.' At moments he found
himself wondering why people around him seemed so upset or
why they put on such solemn faces to talk of what had
happened. At other times, without warning, the sense of loss
would sweep over him. The fact that it was suicide gave the
event an additional dimension of horror: the thought of what
his friend must have been through in those last hours. But it did
not radically alter the basic fact that his friend was dead, that
he would never see him or talk to him again.

* * * * *

Many feelings passed through him in the days before the funeral. Anger, at times: Why did he do this? Do it to me? And after we had talked so often about suicide and agreed that it represented everything we most firmly rejected? Perhaps, he thought, when he agreed with me, when we seemed most to understand each other, he was holding back, not revealing his reservations? Perhaps the belief that there had been any real understanding between them was an illusion? Certainly he now saw that he understood very little about his friend. True, there had been suicide attempts in the past, but they had happened a long time before they met. In the previous few years, and especially in the previous few months, his friend had seemed to recognise that he had a great deal to give to others as a teacher, a writer, a person — and that in this giving a meaning would certainly be found for life. To deny this, to kill himself, was surely a sign that he rejected the validity of all they had talked about, rejected, in a sense, the very basis of their friendship. He felt it was a form of betrayal.

There was anger too at a more trivial level: How could you do this to your friends? How could you force them to clean up after you like this? You who had been so considerate to others all your life? And there was much to clean up: his room to empty, his clothes to sort out, his books to pack, his manuscripts and documents to file away. In that room the futility of it all swept over him: everything so carefully designed for living, for going forward, and then this abrupt end. It made no sense, and despite himself he was furious with his friend for having imposed this upon him.

But such anger could not last long in the face of what had happened. He sensed, moreover, that it was only another manifestation of guilt. For after a suicide everyone feels guilty.

Everyone knows he could have done more — in general terms and also on specific occasions. It is these occasions which are recalled with the same painful insistence as one passes one's tongue again and again over an aching tooth. And the guilt is of course always deserved. We never do enough, always turn away, draw back, refuse to give. There are times, naturally, when we do give, and plentifully, but they never make up for the others, when we don't. If only, we say. If only I had done this, said that, listened more attentively, stretched out a hand. If only.

He had more than his fair share of guilt, for in those last months he had been so caught up in his own affairs that he had felt he was neglecting his friend. Yet friendship ought to be able to survive that. It should be based on the certain knowledge that even if at times the other withdraws, turns away, he is really always there. In times of need he is always there. And the fact was that in a time of need the dead man had turned to none of his friends.

Such guilt is inevitable. But it is also an indulgence. It has more than a hint of masochism about it. He reasoned, as others did, that he had done much, more perhaps than might have been expected, for the dead man. It was an error to dwell upon what he had not done. He would suppress the guilt as he would suppress the anger. Neither was worthy of him or of his friend. And yet they both persisted. In time, he thought, they will go away. But the thoughts would not be suppressed: If only I had done this. Not done that. Been more aware. Less blind. If only. If only.

But even guilt faded a little in the face of sorrow. When he thought of his friend, of what his life must have been like for him to do what he had done, sorrow and pain overwhelmed him, he mourned for the loss of someone with such qualities of spirit and intellect, a good man, a good friend. For the loss of someone whose life, in the previous six years, had grown so closely intertwined with his own. He would no longer come striding into the house for lunch on Sundays. No longer walk over the Downs on long rambles and short walks, with dogs or without. No longer be there to discuss ideas with, to show his work to, to thrust books at. He would no longer be there.

Yet even sorrow is not an emotion that should be cultivated. Like guilt, it is ultimately selfish: he mourned the loss of someone whose presence had afforded him pleasure, but in doing so was he not merely mourning the loss to himself of a part of the world? Such sorrow is easy to indulge in but it is very destructive. It leads nowhere. He wanted to suppress it, but it clung to him. He felt trapped and helpless, unable to move forward or turn round and go back, drained of energy and drowning in guilt and self-pity.

When he became aware of this he decided that the only solution was to go away somewhere and think through the implications of his discovery. He understood that it was essential for his own good to try and grasp what the death of his friend really meant, to him and in itself. He decided to leave as soon as the funeral was over.

\* \* \* \* \*

At the funeral he was numb. There had been too much talk in the previous few days. He had ceased to feel. Others broke down around him or bore up bravely. For him it was merely a day to be got through. He did not believe in funerals or in churches or in the Christian notion of an afterlife. He merely welcomed the event as bringing a time of speculation and uncertainty to some kind of end, as though his friend would only be truly dead once the funeral had taken place. Yet twice in the course of the service he felt a quickening of his interest, a flow of feeling running through him. The first time was at the sudden confrontation with long-familiar words: 'We brought nothing into the world, neither may we take anything out of this world. The Lord giveth and the Lord taketh away. Even as it pleases the Lord, so cometh it to pass: blessed be the name of the Lord.'

He did not know why this stirred him as it did; he only registered with some surprise that it did so. He was, however, far more violently shaken by a prayer spoken by the priest later in the service and taken, he afterwards learnt, from a sermon of John Donne: 'They shall awake as Jacob did, and say as Jacob said, *Surely the Lord is in this place*, and *this is no other but the house of God, and the gate of heaven*. And into that gate they shall enter, and in that house they shall dwell, where there shall be no cloud nor sun, no darkness nor dazzling, but one equal light, no noise nor silence, but one equal music, no fears nor hopes, but one equal possession, no foes nor friends, but one equal communion and identity, no ends nor beginnings, but one equal eternity...'

Not since that first telephone call, when his friend's mother had broken the news to him, had he felt words dropping as these did, straight through him to the centre of his body. And he sensed that they too, like those others, would remain there, alien presences, demanding to be understood and stubbornly resisting understanding.

＊ ＊ ＊ ＊ ＊

He went to the mountains, to a quiet hotel where he would be able to walk and think and write in peace, away from the telephone and the mail and the constant intrusion of those who meant well. It had grown in his mind that what he needed to do was write an elegy for his friend, a memorial that would be both a token of their friendship and the means of coming to terms with what had occurred.

He felt, obscurely, that what was needed was a ceremonious, ritualised piece, in which the personal would gradually be extinguished and reality — the reality of death, of his friend, of his own relation to death, to his friend, and to the death of his friend — would gradually emerge. But as soon as he sat down to write he found himself involved in failure and betrayal. What he wanted was to try and make sense of a specific, a unique event, the single irremediable fact of his friend's death. But as soon as he began to write that death turned into literature, another story, well or badly told, as the case might be, but still one story among thousands. Yet what he wanted, why he was writing, was to make himself understand that this was not just another story, that this was final, irrevocable, once and for all. And to say this was not enough. It merely turned the enterprise into a slightly more sophisticated story. He had wanted to use art to honour his friend and instead found himself using his friend's death as a prop for his art.

As so often in his struggle to emerge from the cotton wool of the self into the clearer order of art — for what was art if not a clearer order? — he tried to start with the immediate: with the cloud of anguish and confusion which lay so heavily upon him. But for once a solution failed to emerge. He was trapped in the cotton wool. He could not put a sentence down without questions of style, of selection, of appropriateness, thrusting themselves upon him. He did not want to write more beautifully, more euphoniously, he wanted only to get at the reality of what had happened. But that reality would remain hidden until he found the right words, and each time he rewrote a passage, scratched out a phrase, the futility of the whole business overcame him. More than futility, betrayal.

For example, to begin with something so fundamental he would not normally think about it at all, it would merely come with the first intense desire to write — in what guise should he himself appear? It would seem natural in the circumstances to use the first person; but that would in fact frustrate his efforts before he had even begun, since it would leave him lumbered with his own selfhood, his own confusions, his own inability to understand, when the object of the whole exercise was precisely to escape from that into a truer understanding of what had happened. Otherwise there would be no need to write except as an act of piety, and piety he had no time for. On the other hand, to use the impersonal 'he' threatened to turn the entire event into a story before he had even begun. It is true that it might be possible to use the 'he' in such a way as to suggest that what was essentially not a story had inevitably to turn into one before it could be told, and the reader might perhaps be driven by the clanging objectivity of the 'he' into an awareness of the unsayable truth. But this was a poor and desperate solution to the problem, and for a while he toyed with the idea of using the second person: that hortatory 'you' would perhaps act as some kind of spiritual tin-opener, prising up the lid of his consciousness as he was writing, forcing him into a clearer apprehension of the truth. However, he soon came to the conclusion that this was far too self-conscious and literary a device. Much more than the other two, it would draw the reader's attention to the work and to its author instead of making him focus more lucidly on the event he wished to illuminate.

Nor was this question of the personal pronoun the only one. Whether he decided to present himself as 'I' or as 'he', there was still the problem of situating himself in relation to his friend. His friend had made an end, had found a place where time and space coincided for him at last. But what end can there be for a memory or a lament? And what part of space can the survivors be said to occupy? Where am I? he thought, in relation to the dead man and to the elegy I want to write? Am I on my knees in church, on a bench looking out at sea, sitting at my desk or lying in bed? Whose mouth is it that says these words, whose hand writes them out? And with that the whole question of the pronouns was upon him again, and the cloud and the cotton wool and the unappeased anguish.

It was in this mood that the words of Donne's sermon came back into his mind: 'And into that gate they shall enter, and in that house they shall dwell, where there shall be no cloud nor sun, no darkness nor dazzling, but one equal light, no noise nor silence, but one equal music, no fears nor hopes, but one equal possession, no foes nor friends, but one equal communion and identity, no ends nor beginnings, but one equal eternity.' He spoke the words over to himself. Again, as when he had first heard them, spoken by the priest at the funeral, he seemed to be on the point of understanding something of great importance, but again, when he made an effort to grasp what that might be, the feeling vanished, the words grew dead.

The cloud settled again. He knew that the only way to dispel it was to write that elegy for his friend, but he knew too that as soon as he tried to think or write he was only allowing the cloud to settle more firmly upon him.

Death, he thought, creates a vacuum into which meanings and emotions rush. And when that death is suicide the process is accelerated a hundredfold. After a suicide everyone finds a dozen explanations of why it happened. No explanation is any more convincing than any other, we feel them all to be inadequate, yet we cannot bear to let the event pass into our memory without giving it some explanation. But because he had felt that every such explanation was only partial, the light it appeared to shed only an illusion, he refused to play the game. In the same way, sensing the inadequacy and partiality of his feelings of anger, of guilt, of sorrow, he had tried to suppress them. But now he wondered if such a suppression of what was after all a natural reaction had not been an error. To deny oneself the freedom to find a meaning in an event because one knows one can never find the real meaning, to deny one's immediate feelings of guilt or sorrow expression because they are selfish and probably self-destructive — was that not perhaps to surround the central event with too much darkness, too much silence? The thousand partial meanings, the confused and sloppy emotions, would lurk in that darkness, in that silence, unable to emerge but also unable to disappear. Perhaps what was needed was not to suppress explanations or emotions because they were false or selfish but, on the contrary, to track them down into the furthest reaches, the darkest corners of the self, and bring them to light. After that the second step, equally essential, could be taken. Once the meanings and the feelings had been recognised, noted and accepted, then it would be possible to eradicate them, extinguish them, burn them out in their entirety. For if too much silence is an error then so is too much noise; if too much darkness then so is too much light. Without the first step the second was impossible; without the second the first would indeed be mere self-indulgence.

But how was this second step to be undertaken? He now

saw that it was precisely here that art came in. The process of
extinction would in fact be one with the process of revelation.
The work of art would bring to light what had previously lain
in darkness and in so doing would reveal it for what it was:
partial, confused, blind, egotistical. But by making what had
hitherto been silent speak it would make it burst and vanish.
Once written out, neither explanations nor meanings would any
longer remain behind to haunt.

The impulse of art, he now understood, is right: the impulse
towards a form, towards the articulation of pain and loss. But
while recognising this we should also recognise the falsehood
inherent in such articulation. To speak it, to write it, is always
to get it wrong. But to understand our distance from understanding is also a form of understanding. To grasp our inability
to pay our true respects to the dead is perhaps a form of respect.
Our art, it is true, clouds or dazzles, deafens with too much
noise or too much silence, distorts reality with its beginnings
an endings. Yet, if we will let it, it can also make manifest that
which it cannot express.

We have witnessed an event. In this our life we will perhaps
never be anything other than witnesses, even when the event is
our own death. For what are we? We came into this world with
nothing and we will leave it with nothing. Are we synonymous
with our possessions? Clearly not. With our thoughts? No.
With our language? No. We borrow words from the common
stock in order to talk about ourselves and too often forget that
the 'our' in that expression is only a manner of speaking. Of
ourselves we are nothing, no 'I' or 'he' or even 'you'; only a
potential that can be stirred into life by such impersonal activ-
ities as games or art, praise or lament. Through the gradual
extinction of the mythical self to which we cling so blindly, of

'I' and 'you' and 'he', of anger and guilt and sorrow, we arrive not at a lifeless husk but at its radiant opposite, an animate potential which includes the dead as well as the living, where (for a moment) you are Alan as well as me, and I can be the three of us and you and I understand that this is both true and not true and that in this understanding, at long last, there is no darkness and no dazzling but one equal light, no noise and no silence but one equal music, no fears nor hopes but one equal possession, no foes nor friends but one equal communion and identity, no ends and no beginnings but one equal eternity.

\* \* \* \* \*

He stopped in the silence of the hotel room and looked up from his page. Then he bent his head again and read over what he had written. For a moment, in the act of writing, he had thought he had succeeded at last in what he had set out to do. Now, reading it through, he realised that it was only another failure; and it was small comfort to him to understand as well that it was also the nearest he would ever come to success in this particular enterprise.

# Brothers

He climbs the stairs. I know him by his tread. My brother! The door creaks a little as he pushes it. Now he steps inside and says hello. He stands by the door and looks round. What a funny place to be, he says. Not the house, he adds. The house is very nice. Very nice indeed, as far as I can judge. But why do you sit here in the dusk like that? I knew it was you, I tell him. He comes forward into the room. There is nowhere for him to sit. There is only the table in the middle of the room, with its chair, and I am already sitting on the chair. He walks to the window and leans against the sill. I knew it was you, I tell him. I know your tread. I called, he says. I knocked. I only let myself in when no one answered. I tell him I heard someone call, but it seemed a long way off, and then there was silence, broken only by a dog barking in the distance. He repeats what a nice house it is and how well I have done for myself and how quiet and secluded it is. I almost could not get through because of the snow, he says. He asks me to return with him, he asks me to cease to turn my head away from things and come back. I explain to him that back has no meaning for me. He insists that it is nothing to do with my wife, that that is entirely my own affair, that he has

come of his own accord, that he cannot let me do this to myself.
It upsets him that I do not respond to this. I tell him about the
snow. I tell him how I wake thinking I am lying in the snow, a
black figure on the white hillside, and I have just been dreaming
that I am in my clean bare room at the top of the house and
have received a visit from my brother. I am lying in the snow
and yet I can still feel myself in the room, deep in conversation
with my brother. The ties between us are so close that it is not
a matter of what we say at all. He does not want me to break
free as I have done, it makes him feel imprisoned in the web of
his own commitments. But it also makes him feel anxious for
my sake, more anxious than he would be for his own. The two
things, the envy and the concern, cannot be disentangled, either
on his side or on mine. When I tell him about the snow and
the cold hillside and the dawn he grows angry, waves his arms,
tells me not to be silly. I ask him if he is not ever prone to such
imaginings himself, if driving down in his car for instance he
did not at moments think himself in my place, even perhaps
imagine himself lying in the snow, inert, with a dog barking at
this black unmoving shape, and if it was not perhaps something
of a relief to feel that it was all over, at last. He does not answer.
He looks out of the window, at the woods and the hills beyond
and the snow on the hills. He repeats that enough is enough,
that I have made my point and now I should come back. I never
thought you would do it, he says, you talked about it so much.
He assures me he has not come as an emissary from my wife,
though she does of course need me and would welcome me
back, to say nothing of the children. He tells me it is entirely
on his own initiative that he has come, that he drove in the early
hours, when all of London was still asleep, and kept on driving
until he reached me. Now he has come to take me back. I am

not sure that this is really what he has come for. I wonder if it is not to talk about himself, to ask my advice, to tell me that he needs my help in order to escape from the life that has trapped him. You turn your head away, he says. You refuse to listen. I tell him that I am glad he is here, that in some obscure way I have been waiting for his tread on the stair, that I have often, since I have come here, imagined this scene between us in the long, bare, low-ceilinged room, that it is as if we had always been here, together, talking. He interrupts me to say that I always turn the specific into the general, that I dissolve one thing into another and so evade decisions. He repeats that I must return with him, that I cannot do what I have done. I know that he is waiting for me to persuade him, that it would disappoint him deeply were I to accede to his request and return with him, though in another way of course it would please him, it would show him that he was the stronger and more decisive of us two.

And of course he is also genuinely concerned about me, he is worried to see me alone, sitting at a table in the dusk in the middle of an empty room, at the top of an empty house, doing nothing. I could of course return with him, merely to show myself that I am strong enough for anything, that I am not cowering here out of fear of the world. Yet to do so would be a show of weakness rather than strength. I really have no need of him. I have my house and my table and my chair and I have turned my head away from all the rest, as he so rightly observes, so there is an end to it. He has perched himself on the sill of the window in a rather awkward way, and now waits for me to reply. I tell him about my walks in the snow. I tell him how as I sit here at the table in the middle of an empty room I some-times feel with absolute clarity that I am lying in the snow, one hand flung out, the other over my heart. A dog barks nearby, barks at this prostrate form, but I do not move. The dog's bark grows more and more distant. I am lying in the snow but at the same time I am sitting in my quiet room in the dusk, and I hear the tread of my brother's footsteps on the stairs. I wait for him to enter. He pushes the door open a little and it creaks as he does so, then he is inside the room and we are talking as we have always talked. I ask him if he is not subject to such fantasies. He turns his back to me and looks out of the window. He wants me to cease this nonsense. He wants me to return to my family, my home, my job. He wants me to stay here, he is proud of me for doing what I have done. So it has always been between us. He drives his little car along the motorway with the snow piled up on either side and in his mind's eye he can see me sitting in the dusk at my table in the middle of the empty room, he can see me lying on the hillside, a dark figure, one hand flung out and the other over his heart. He approaches and bends over me. His legs are stiff from all the driving he has had to do that day. He looks into my face, and as he does so he realises it is himself he is looking at. That is what our lives have always been like, entangled one with the other to the point sometimes of total confusion. That is why we have got on so badly. As he drives he is lying out on the hillside, his body is growing cold. A dog has seen the prostrate form and barks in a fury of anxiety. I have died in peace, he thinks, my brother at least did not try to pester me, did not attempt to pull me back. He did not drive down in his little car and try to persuade me to return. Perhaps there is, for a moment, just a hint of resentment at his brother for not doing so, a feeling, fleetingly experienced, that if he is now dying like this in the snow it is his brother's fault for making no move to save him from himself. But that is quickly dissipated in the larger sense of peace. For his brother has come, after all, there is his tread on the stair. I sit in my room, he thinks, and there is my brother, after all. My heart fills with joy. He has come! In a minute he will be in the room with me. He has driven all the way down from London setting out when it was still dark and driving for hours through the snow-covered countryside. Now he is here, with me, talking. It does not matter what we say to each other. It is only important that he is here. He checks to see how many miles he has done since he left the house and returns to imagining what it will be like when he arrives. Perhaps this time, he thinks, I will know how I really feel towards him. Perhaps I will suddenly understand if it is pity or envy I feel towards him. The dog barks but now there is no one to hear it. It draws near to the prostrate form and sniffs, then utters a howl and backs away. My brother turns from the window. Please, he says. It is I who need you. When he says that my heart warms towards him. It does not matter what words pass between us. What matters is that he is here, with me, in the big, bare, low-ceilinged room, and that we are talking.

# Christmas

Frank, the father, is waiting at the station.

— What's all this? he says.

— Don't worry, the son says, I haven't come to stay.

— I didn't think for a moment that you had, the father says. I was just —

— Careful! It's fragile.

— What is it?

— You'll see.

He gets into the passenger seat and the father starts the car. — You're looking well, he says.

— Am I?

— In the circumstances.

— Yeah.

Frank has not known his son so silent. — How's Timothy? he asks.

— Shit, Dad, his son says. Don't *make conversation*.

— I just asked.

— OK.

They are silent until he pulls into the drive and brings the car to a stop. They get out.

— No, his son says, I'll handle it. It's delicate.

– What is it?

– Nothing. I'll show you later.

– I'm intrigued.

– It's just something I'm making for Tim.

– What sort of thing?

– Oh, a Noah's Ark.

– A Noah's Ark? What are you talking about?

– It's a school project.

– A Noah's Ark?

– Uhuh.

The father leads the way. – I've put you in your old room, he says. Or would you rather have the usual?

– Whatever.

Now he can see his son in a good light he finds he isn't looking all that well after all.

– I just thought you wouldn't want the double bedroom now you...

– Whatever, his son says.

– I thought it might bring back memories and...

– Don't be so damned *sensitive,* his son says. And then go *on* about it.

They stand in the doorway of the small bedroom.

– So that I'll say: *sensitive!* his son says angrily.

– I'm sorry, he says. Your mother always stopped me. She kept me from making a fool of myself.

– Oh, Dad, for God's sake! his son says. Just get out of the room and let me unpack.

– Sorry.

– Just get out, Dad, his son says. Just get out.

\*  \*  \*  \*  \*

— Hey! the son says as he comes into the kitchen. A fire. Great!

    — I thought we could eat in here, Frank says. I don't use the dining room much any more.

    — I like it here, the son says. It feels good.

    — We always had a fire in here, Frank says. When your mother was alive. Remember?

    — It's great, the son says. I've brought you some single malt, he says, putting the bottle down on the kitchen table.

    — I don't drink any more.

    — You don't? Why not?

    — I'm afraid.

    — What of?

    — That I might not be able to stop. Now I'm by myself.

    — Oh, come off it, Dad, his son says.

    — I've cooked something nice for us this evening.

    — That's good. Mind if I have a glass?

    — Of course not. Do you want something with it?

But his son has already opened the bottle.

    — Ice? Frank says. Water?

    — No no, his son says

They sit at the kitchen table.

After a while his son says: — You don't want to see it?

    — What?

    — The Noah's Ark

    — Of course. Bring it down.

    — It's a bit big. You come and see it.

They climb the stairs.

    — Is the room all right? the father asks.

    — Of course. Why?

    — I don't know. Your mother dealt with all that sort of thing.

— What sort of thing?

— Allotting rooms to guests. Making beds and so forth.

— It's not very difficult, is it?

— No. But I was afraid I might have forgotten something. So, he says, squatting down on the floor to get a closer look. This is it.

— It's a project, the son says. They all have to make something.

— Why are you doing it for him then?

— I'm not doing it. I'm only helping. It's his idea and everything.

— So they don't all have to do an ark?

— No no. Whatever they want.

— What gave him the idea?

— He likes animals.

— There aren't any animals.

— They're too difficult to do and then fit in. This is the ark before the animals came in.

— I see, Frank says.

— He likes boats too.

— I know, Frank says.

— I thought it might be because it was the first bit of carpentry and all that, he says after a while.

— What do you mean?

— It's in the Bible.

— I know it's in the Bible!

— I mean no one except God ever made anything before that.

— Really?

— Why did you bring it down with you? Frank asks.

— I still have a few things to do to it. And I thought if I had time I might start painting it.

— You're painting it?

— Yes. Why not? A nice red. Make it stand out.

— Red?

— Why not?

— I don't know. I thought... Do you want to use the garage?

— The garage?

— To paint it?

— Can we go downstairs? his son says. When's dinner? I'm hungry.

— It's almost ready. It's pretty basic. Your mother did all the cooking.

— For God's sake, Dad! his son says. She's been dead three years.

— What difference does that make?

— Don't go *on* about it! his son says.

\* \* \* \* \*

The son reaches across the table and pulls the bottle of wine to him.

— Sorry, Frank says. Help yourself.

— I still can't believe it, his son says. I still don't know what happened.

The father is silent.

— I know she still loves me, his son says. I can hear it in her voice on the phone.

— Give her time, Frank says.

— Time! his son says. She's living with this guy. She's chosen him over me. I can't believe it.

He pours himself another glass of wine.

— These things happen, his father says.

— I didn't think they'd happen to me.

— You haven't met anyone else? his father asks

— Dad, the son says. I love her. She loves me. It doesn't make any sense.

— We've got to play the cards we're dealt, his father says. Look at me.

— Shit, Dad, the son says. You're old. Mother was old. She died. She loved you. How can you compare the two things?

— I'm not comparing, his father says. I wouldn't compare a death to a marital problem.

— Fuck you, Dad, his son says. You insist I come down for Christmas, and then you give me this shit? Is there another bottle somewhere?

— I thought we should be together at a time like this, his father says, getting up to fetch another bottle. Families should stick together at Christmas.

— Here, give it to me, his son says, taking the bottle and corkscrew from him.

He pours himself another glass. — I try to hate her, he says. For what she's done to me. To Tim. But I can't. I love her, Dad. And I know she loves me too, only she's got this thing into her head and...

— Give her time, his father says. She'll come back.

— I don't want her back, the son says. Not after what she's done to me.

— Then what do you want?

— I want to die, his son says.

His father is silent, staring at him across the table.

He gets up and clears away the plates. — Shall we keep the Christmas pudding till tomorrow? he asks.

— Whatever, his son says.

— Perhaps we'd better, the father says.

— Whatever, the son says.

— It's a difficult time, the father says. The darkest time of the year. That's why families get together and everyone eats as much as they can, isn't it? You'll feel better as soon as the days start getting longer.

— You know what I did last summer? his son says. After she left? I never even drew the curtains. I couldn't stand all that light and the thought of everybody else having a good time. I couldn't stand it.

The father is silent.

— I'd rather kill myself than have another summer like the last, the son says.

— Don't talk like that.

— How do you want me to talk then? You and Mum always taught me to speak openly about what I felt. And now I'm doing so, you try to shut me up.

— I'm not trying to shut you up, the father says. I just feel such talk is pointless. You only talk yourself into a depression.

— I'm not depressed, his son says, filling his glass again. I just can't see why I should live any more. I can't face twenty-four hours every day and sixty minutes to the hour and sixty seconds to the minute. I see her all the time. I see her with this guy and I see her with me and I hear her voice calling as she used to do when she got home. That's all, Dad. Do you understand? That's all.

— It's supposed to be a time of hope, his father says. The birth of the Christ child and all that.

His son is silent.

— You've got Tim to worry about, so stop being so self-centred, he says.

— That's rich, the son says. That's rich, coming from you.

— What do you mean? Frank says.

His son drains his glass and refills it.

— The trouble with you, his father says, is that we gave you too much love. Now you expect the same from everyone. But you can't get it. Life's not like that. She probably couldn't stand things any more with you, for whatever reason. These things aren't rational, you know. She just felt she had to leave.

— We loved each other, the son says. What there was between us was something I haven't seen among any of the couples I know. I understood her. I understood what made her tick. And she understood me, Dad. It doesn't make sense. Is there another bottle of this?

— Don't you think we should go to bed? his father says.

— And do what? his son says.

The father is silent. Then he says: — You're eaten up with self-pity.

— Perhaps I am, his son says.

The father suddenly feels a rush of love for his son. He gets up and goes round the table. He puts his arms round his shoulders.

— Oh, Dad, stop it, the son says, squirming.

— It'll be all right, Frank says. Whatever happens it'll be all right.

His son pushes his arm away and pours himself another drink.

— I think I'll turn in now, he says.

— Do that, Frank says. Try and get a good night's sleep.

— I've got things to do, his son says. I'm not going to sleep.

— What things?

— Things, his son says. He gets up from the table and weaves his way to the door.

— I thought we might have a walk tomorrow, his father says. Get over to the cliffs.

— Goodbye Dad, his son says, turning at the door.

— Goodnight, Frank says.

\* \* \* \* \*

He sits on at the table, listening to his son padding about in the room above. The afternoon and evening have taken it out of him and he finds himself sinking into a doze, still at the table. Finally he hears his son fall heavily on the bed and after that there is a silence.

Turned from the table, he gazes into the fire.

And then he hears it. Plip plip plip plip. He realises he's been hearing it for some time. At once it comes to him. It's drops. On the carpet. He looks up at the ceiling.

A red spot, blotchy, of uneven outline, is clearly visible half-way between the light bulb and the wall. As he watches he sees a red drop form and then slowly detach itself and fall with the now expected noise onto the carpet. Even as it does so another drop has formed and followed it, and then another and another.

Hardly able to breathe, clutching his heart, the father stares at the mark on the ceiling.

— Oh God! he says.

He stumbles to the door and climbs the stairs. His legs are so heavy he has to drag himself up by clinging to the banisters. He is aware of how silent the house suddenly is.

On the landing he steadies himself, then pushes open the door of his son's room.

His son is lying, fully clothed, on the bed, one foot still on the floor. The sound of his snores fills the room.

On the floor, by the little wooden boat, a tin of red paint is lying on its side, slowly disgorging its contents onto the carpet.

– Oh God! the father whispers. Oh God! You bastard! You absolute fucking bastard!

# That Which Is Hidden Is That Which Is Shown; That Which Is Shown Is That Which Is Hidden

One day they found him under the bed, curled tight, pressed against the wall. For as long as they could remember he had been in the habit of hiding objects in boxes, in drawers, in holes he dug in the garden. Sometimes, when they sat down to a meal after calling for him in vain, he would suddenly appear from under the table. But when they found him that day under the bed it was different. He wouldn't come out, and they had to pull the bed aside and haul him to his feet. His pockets were stuffed with objects: pebbles, a rusty spoon, two pen-knibs, a half-sucked sweet. When they asked him what he was up to he wouldn't reply. They pleaded, threatened, cajoled. When they finally gave up he went back to his place under the bed.

He was no trouble at school, did his homework, bothered no one. But he began to spend more and more time in cupboards, sitting in the dark, or crouched in a corner of the pantry, behind the potatoes. In the attic they found an inlaid mother-of-pearl box with a cricket ball nestling inside. When they tackled him about it he only shook his head, so they desisted, and hoped the fad would pass.

No one ever complained of him, but he was not interested in his work at school and left as soon as he could. He was never a burden to them, was never out of work, though he rarely held down any job for very long. One day he disappeared, and when he turned up again he told them he had found a room nearer his work.

In his new room he fitted out a workbench and began to make little boxes for himself out of bits of wood he found lying in dumps, and then more elaborate things, cupboards, boats, mysterious contraptions with shelves and holes and little passages and conduits linking one part of the interior to another. Inside these spaces and holes stood little wooden men, sometimes with trays in their hands, staring straight ahead of them, birds with beady eyes, giraffes. The door into the dark spaces was always half open, so that the figure was both concealed and revealed. Look, he said to his mother. Look, look inside. And closed the little door.

The objects proliferated, grew more complex. He gave up his job and concentrated on his craft. He spent hours walking the streets, looking for likely pieces of wood. Sometimes he took trips to the seaside and collected hard grainy driftwood. Back in his room he sawed and chiselled and sandpapered. He used no nails, only wooden pins he made himself. The objects, looking like a cross between old butter-churns and complicated toys, stood in rows against the walls of his room. There is nothing inside them, he said to his father. And held the little door closed. Nothing inside.

The room is empty now. He has gone, taking his possessions with him. In a derelict house, not far from the station, the police have found a number of strange objects: little cabinets with multiple divisions, and, here and there, behind half-open doors, tiny wooden figures, round-eyed, staring straight ahead in the dark. The house is crumbling, deserted. The police take away the objects and then, when no one claims them, smash them up and throw them away.

There are no objects any more. There were never any objects. Now you know. Don't look for me. By the time you read this I will be far away. You will never find me.

# A Changeable Report

KENT: Report is changeable.
*King Lear*, IV.vii.92

*To Nick Woodeson*

I have been dead for five years. I say dead and I am trying to be as precise as possible. I do not know how else to put it. My hand trembles as I write but it is comforting to have pen and ink and paper on which to write things down. It is as if I had forgotten how to use a pen. I have to pause before each word. Sometimes I cannot remember how a word is spelled. Sometimes I cannot remember how the letters are formed. But it is a comfort to bend over the white page and think about these things. If I could explain what happened I might find myself alive once more. That is the most terrible thing. The thing I really hate them for. They have taken away my life, though no court of law would convict them for it. When I think about that time and what they did to me my insides get knotted up in anger and despair and I hate them not so much for what they did then as for what they are doing to me now, knotting me up with anguish and hatred at the memory.

I have tried to understand what happened. I thought that if I could put it all down on paper I would finally understand and I would be free of them for ever. But when I try I cannot continue. There is a darkness all round the edges. I think that by writing I will be able to shift that darkness a little, allow light to fall on the central events at least. But it does not work like that. It is as though the light follows each letter, each word perhaps, but no more, and in doing so moves away from the previous word, which is once again swallowed up in darkness. I pinch myself to make myself concentrate. I bite my lips and try to look as steadily as possible at what has occurred, at what is occurring. But the light moves along with the pen and I can never hold more than a small sequence in my mind at any one time. So I give up and wait for a better moment. But there is no better moment. There is just the urge to seize the pen again and write.

I did not think writing was so important. Till they shut me up. There was no cause. I had been gulled. But they bundled me in and locked the door. They told me I was mad. In the dark I felt about for windows, candles, but there were none. I was afraid of suffocating. I have always been afraid of that. I used to have nightmares about being shut into a basket and forgotten. I could hear them outside, chattering and laughing. I asked for pen and paper. I had to write and tell her what they had done to me. When they finally let me do so she had me released at once. I did not think I had changed then. I did not realise what it does to you to be shut up in the dark without hope or the ability to keep track of time. I vowed revenge on the whole pack of them. As I left I heard him start to sing. I went out into the night.

I had never had much time for his songs or his silly repartees. I do not know why she put up with him. Or with any of them. I need my sleep. I did my work well. I tried to keep them under control. I asked for nothing more. The noise they made. I could not stand that noise, that drunken bawling at all hours of the day and night. I cannot stand the sight of grown men who have deliberately befuddled themselves. It is degrading. Besides, she paid me to keep order in the house and I kept order as best I could. She should never have indulged him. Why put up with even a cousin if he consistently behaves like that? Why keep a Fool just because your father kept one? A hateful habit, demeaning to both parties. Let the Spaniards retain the custom, they are little better than beasts themselves. But that she should do so! And a foolish Fool at that. A knave. As bad as the rest of them, Maria and the cousin and his idiot friend. The noise they made. The songs they sang. Obscene. Meaningless. Vapid. Why did she let them? If it had been me I would soon have sent them packing. Restored some decency to the house. And her still in mourning for her brother.

I thought she had more sense. A page. A mere boy. Get him into bed at any cost. Forget her brother. Forget the injunctions of her father. What kind of life do humans want to lead, what kind of a –

My stomach has knotted up again. I hate them for making me hate in this way. I hate them for doing this to me. When I walked out into the night he was singing about the wind and the rain. I thought I would be revenged on them all. My stomach was knotted with anger. I wanted to scream, to kick and punch them, him especially. Toby, the fat cousin, the –

I have said to myself that I will keep calm. I have promised myself that I will control myself and write it all down so that I may understand and be free of the darkness. I am a survivor. I

have not survived this long without learning a little about how
it is done. I have the will, I have the patience. They think only
of the moment. They drink and joke and sing. They did this to
me. They tried to make me mad. They could not bear to have
me there, watching them, I —

At moments, as I write, I no longer know who I am. It feels
as though all this had happened to someone else and it had
simply been reported to me. I see things in my head. My
stomach knots in pain and anger. But I am not sure if my head
and my stomach belong to the same person.

Never mind. I must use what skills I have and not be
deflected. I must be patient. Men have burrowed out of
dungeons with nothing but a nail-file. What are five years or
ten when life itself is at stake? I have always been patient. I have
my pen and paper and I can always start again. And again and
again until the darkness is dispersed and I can emerge into the
light once more and live.

I remember the man I was. But he is like a puppet. I do not
know what kept him going. Perhaps it was nothing except a
sense of duty. I see him bustle. He was a great bustler. I sometimes think I am still there. That I still work there, do what I
have to do about the house, take orders from him, from the boy
now, while she stands simpering by. I hate her for that, for what
she let them do to me and for standing by now and doting on
that boy.

But I am not there. I know I am not there. I turned my back
on them forever and walked out, vowing revenge. Yet I was not
interested in revenge. I only wanted to forget them. To start
again elsewhere. But I could not. The song would not let me
go. It was like a leash he had attached to me when he saw that
I was determined to go. I sleep and it comes to me in my dreams.

I wake and it creeps up on me in the daytime. I plotted revenge. I thought I would find my way back there and take up my post with them again. I would steal her handkerchief and poison his mind. He would have killed her for that. Killed her first and then himself. He was capable of it, he went for Andrew the minute he saw him, broke his head and then blamed Toby. They would have taken me back. I know how she felt about me. I would have played on those feelings. I would have made him kill her and then, in despair, he would have done away with himself.

At other moments I thought of other, sillier kinds of revenge. I would have them all on an island. I would be able to control the wind and the waves. I would wreck them on my island. The drunken idiots would be pinched and bruised and bitten by spirits, and the others, the others would get their deserts — the whole lot of them. I would frighten them with ghosts made of old sheets, I would lead them into swamps and then reveal myself to them — it would be the silliness of the punishments that would be the most shaming.

Idle thoughts. I am surprised that I can remember them. At moments they were there, so strong, so clearly formulated. But I do not think I ever took them seriously. Because it was as if I had lost the ability to act. As if his song had drained me of my will. When it flooded through my head I cried. I cried a lot. There was another music too, unearthly, and fragments of speeches, but not speeches in the ordinary sense. I understood what they said, but not the meaning of the individual words and phrases. It was as though their souls had found words. In such a night, was the refrain. The names of Cressida and of Dido, of Thisbe and of Medea came into it. The floor of heaven like a carpet thick inlaid with patines of bright gold. I remember that.

It was like a music I had never heard before and and never imagined could exist. And then I was in the dark but it was peaceful, quite different from that other dark, and there was another song, fear no more the heat of the sun, and home art gone and ta'en thy wages. It merged with the other voices, telling of Dido and Medea and Thisbe and Cressida. But when I tried to hear them more clearly, to focus on them better, they faded away and vanished altogether. I went out through a door and instead of the garden I had expected there was desert, dirt, an old newspaper blowing across a filthy street, decaying tenements. I turned back and there was the music again, but now the door was locked and I could not get in. Why do I know nothing about music? Why have I always feared it? Not just the drunken catches but the pure sweet music of viols, the pure sweet melancholy songs, I fear them all.

I tried to walk then but my feet kept going through the rotten planks. I put my hand up to my head and the hair came away in clumps. I knew this was not so, I knew it was only my imagination. I fought against it. They are trying to do this to me, I said to myself. They want you to think that you are mad. You will not give them that satisfaction. But I woke up dreaming that my head was made of stone and I held it in my lap, sightless eyes gazing past me into the sky. My daughter had betrayed me. She had stolen all my jewellery and absconded with a Negro. There was a storm and women spoke and tempted me, I looked at my hands and they were covered with blood. The storm grew worse and I was on a deserted heath and howling. An idiot and a blind old man held on to me, trying to pull me down, uttering gibberish, but I kicked them off and there was that song again, about the wind and the rain. In the rain my daughter came and we talked. Something terrible had happened but all was forgiven. She talked to me. She answered when I spoke to her. But I knew it would not last and it didn't, she was dead in my arms, I held her and she weighed less than a cat. I pretended she was alive but I knew she was dead, I walked again and the rotten boards gave way, one leg stuck in the ground, it grew into the ground, and all the time I knew it was not so, that if I could turn, if I could return, and it required so small an effort, so very small an effort, then it would all change, she would be with me on the island and I would rule over the wind and the waves, she had only pretended to run away, only pretended to be dead. But I also knew that I could not make that effort, that I could not go back, that the door was shut forever, hey ho the wind and the rain. I marked the days, the years. I sat at my desk and wrote as well as I could on the white paper. I was determined that they would not make me mad.

It has been like death. Time has not moved at all. Yet it cannot be long before the real thing. I try to put it down as clearly as I can, but there is a darkness behind and in front. Nothing stays still. I cannot illuminate any of it. I form the letters as well as I am able, but I cannot read what I have written. It does not seem to be written in any language that I know. The more I look at it the more incomprehensible it seems to be. As though a spider had walked through the ink and then crawled across the page. As though it had crawled out of my head and on to the paper and there could never be any sense in the marks it had left.

Perhaps there are no marks. Perhaps I am still in the dark and calling out for pen and paper. Perhaps no time at all has passed since they shut me up. I call for pen and ink and paper but they only laugh and cry out that I am mad. I do not know who I am. Except that I am a survivor. I will go on trying to write something down. This is a pen in my hand. I hold it and write with it. This is me, writing. I will not listen to their words. I will not listen to that music. I will try to be as precise as possible. I will write it all down. The darkness will clear. It must clear. The music will fade. It must fade. I will be able to live again. That will be my revenge on them. That I have endured. That I have not let them make me mad.

## Volume IV, pp. 167–69

She was born in a small Austrian village a few miles from Salzburg. Her father was a baker and the smell of warm bread stayed with her to the end. It was not a good time to be born: 1928. She was the only child. Her mother died during the war, of fear and malnutrition. Her father went on baking. In 1946 she entered the University of Vienna. Obscurely, she already knew what her life would be like.

She took a degree in modern languages and then found a job in a big cement factory, dealing with the foreign correspondence. She saw the refugees pouring through Vienna but made no comment. Her stories had begun to appear in student magazines, and then in the more adventurous literary journals, in Berlin as well as Vienna. They were quiet stories, impersonal, level in tone. But their quietness masked an unease; or rather, affected the reader with unease by their very freedom from all sense of it. At the time they were described as 'pure', as 'classically calm', but their very purity seemed somehow to throw doubt upon the very possibility of classicism. All in all, a surprising literary venture in the hectic climate of those postwar years.

After only a few months she left her lodgings near the factory and went to live with a painter. They had known each other at university. He was older than she was and had been married before. Shortly after this she gave up her job, but the greater freedom this allowed her did not seem to affect her writing one way or the other. Her stories continued to appear, at the rate of one, or at most two, a year. Quietly, they made their mark.

Four years, almost to the day, after she had moved in with the painter she paid a visit to her father, the baker. She sat in the back of the shop, as she had done as a child, and watched him at work. Afterwards, they shared a meal. Then she went back to Vienna, packed her bags, and caught the train for Rome.

The painter did not try to follow her. He knew it would not be any use, felt even that somehow, somewhere, he had always known it would happen. From Rome she wrote to him, saying that the absence of German in the air soothed her. 'My words on the white paper always look unreal,' she wrote. 'Now their unreality is justified.' He would have liked her to say 'at least' – 'is at least justified' – but that of course she would never do, 'is justified' was all he could expect from her. Indeed, he would perhaps have been disappointed with anything else.

Her stories grew simpler, purer. As though she would force reality to manifest itself by isolating the very essence of that which it was not. She lived alone, in a small but comfortable flat in Trastevere. Her stories had been published in many countries now. In the German edition they stood, three slim volumes, in elegant off-white covers, on the shelves of all the libraries and bookshops. No one asked if they provided a sufficient income for her to live on and, if not, for it seemed unlikely, how she managed. Her life, like her writings, was as it was. There was no room for questions.

One day there was a fire in the flat. Flames shot out of the windows and on the other floors women screamed in terror. When the firemen eventually succeeded in putting out the blaze very little damage had been done to the building. But in her flat nothing remained but a heap of charred and sodden ruins. And she too was found, burned almost beyond recognition.

Her stories sit on the shelves, four chaste volumes in off-white covers (the fourth was published after her death). In their simplicity and purity they give nothing away. Did she feel the impossible strain of that purity, that calmness? She always knew exactly what she was doing, no one had any doubt of that. She would know when there was nothing more to be said. Some of her friends maintained that violent action went against the whole tenor of her life and beliefs. They pointed to the fact that accident often played a role in her stories, yet accident so calmly rendered as barely to disturb the smooth sequence of seemingly inevitable events which her stories seemed less to create than to coax into visibility before our always myopic gaze. There is no such thing as a dead end, they liked to quote her as saying. When all the roads are blocked there is always another way round. It is merely a question of patience. Patience and attention.

For days, though, the smell of burning hung over the building.

# Exile

When the letter arrived from my sister informing me that she was coming I cannot say that I was altogether happy. Of course I have always been glad to see her. Once we were very close, but when you live as far apart as we have for the past few years it is difficult to keep such a relationship going. I must confess that I could not even, at first, remember what she looked like, and wondered whether I would recognise her at the station. I was surprised too that they had let her come, since in the early days she had moved heaven and earth to be allowed to do so, but without success. Yet now she wrote that she was on her way, and with vital news which she could only impart in person.

Suddenly the little town no longer seemed familiar. I had grown so used to it that I had entirely ceased to notice it, but in the days that followed the arrival of her letter I began to see it as she would see it, and I knew she would have little good to say of it. I tried hard to remember how it had struck me when I had first arrived, but you cannot simply wish away so many thousand days, pretend they have not happened. And the truth is that I had come to terms with the town. With the fact that it had nothing distinctive about it, not a hill or a river or a park even, that it was freezing in winter and, for a few terrible weeks in summer, unbearably hot. With the fact that the inhabitants were taciturn if not actively hostile, as though they had seen too many of us in the past few years and preferred to act as though we were not there. I had also got used to the fact of having nothing to do all day, though at first that was what I had dreaded most of all. I had in effect found a rhythm, a pattern. Every day I walked through the identical streets with their rows of identical houses and identical wooden palings; stopped every now and then to watch children clearing the snow from the tiny front yards; bought the few provisions I needed; returned to the cold flat; cooked; sat huddled against the cold for an hour or two, in the dark, looking out at the moonlit town under its blanket of snow, and tumbled into bed to sleep as best I could. For some reason the satisfaction this programme afforded me was epitomised by a peculiar sensation of peace and well-being, which would run through me sometimes as I lay in bed in the bitter-cold pitch-black early mornings and stretched my legs out to opposite sides of the bed, so that the blanket was pulled taut between the toes of either foot. Curiously, in that moment I would feel, in the intimate core of my body, that I actually existed in this world of silent streets and identical houses, of white skies and dirty snow, in a way I had not known myself to exist before, in the excitement and hurly-burly of the big cities in which I had always lived. And now here was my sister writing that she was arriving, and with news she could hardly wait to impart.

One train a week stops at our little station. It usually brings people here; hardly ever takes anybody away. This is not a place one leaves, either for a short time or for ever. You have to learn to live with that, as you learn to live with everything. And nothing, once learned, can be unlearned. That is the barrier between those of us who have had to settle down here and the rest of the world. It is not something you can convey to someone who has not experienced it for himself. I tried to explain this to my sister, as she sprawled on the bed in my room and I sat on the floor leaning back against the door. But she was not really listening. Her asking me how I was had not meant to entail the kind of lengthy reply I was giving her. She was anxious only to impart the news she had brought with her. In the middle of my attempt to make her understand she said suddenly:

— Listen. You know what I've come to say. You're free.

— Free? I said.

— Yes, she said. Free. You can pack your things and come back with me.

— Don't be ridiculous, I said. Her words didn't make sense. I didn't know which way to take them. From the moment I received her letter I had sensed obscurely that her visit was a mistake.

— Yes, she said. Yes. They rang and told me.

I tried to focus on her face but the room was spinning. This often happens to me in winter, when the cold is a perpetual misery and there is not enough food to stop you always being hungry. Finally I said: — They'd have let me know.

— I was to tell you, she said. You can come back with me. Do you understand? You're free.

I looked hard at her till I had got her completely in focus. Her eyes were gleaming with excitement. She was hugging her knees as she used to do as a child. I have always found it slightly affected in a grown woman, especially one who, like her, is running to plumpness.

— It's true, she said. They even told me you would get your job back.

I laughed. My sister has always been so gullible.

— Don't laugh, she said. It's true. I checked.

— Checked?

— I rang the paper. They said yes, your job was there, waiting for you. They even asked me to give them the exact date when you would be back.

— You're joking, I said.

— Would I come all this way for a joke?

I had to admit she wouldn't.

— Go on, she said. Pack your bags. We're leaving this dump on the next train.

— They're pulling your leg, I said.

— I thought that too at first, she said. I must admit I thought they might be doing that, I wouldn't put it past them. That's why I rang the paper. But no. It's correct. They're just waiting for you there. They told me to tell you.

— They're in on it then, I said. In on the whole thing.

— In on what? she said.

— On the hoax.

For the first time since her arrival she seemed nonplussed. As if she had suddenly realised matters were not as simple as she had imagined.

— Listen, she said. It's true. All you have to do is step on that train with me and you'll see it's true. I've brought money for your ticket, she added, as though that might be a complication.

— It's not true, I repeated. I won't let them do this to me.

— Do what?

— Humiliate me, I said.

— What are you talking about? she said.

I was silent. How could I explain?

– Come on! she said impatiently. It's true I tell you!

I did not look at her. After a while she said quietly: – What do I have to do to persuade you?

– Nothing, I said.

– Oh, she said, relieved. I'm glad.

– I'm not going, I said.

– Not going?

– They're not going to humiliate me, I said. I didn't know why I kept using that word, humiliate.

– What humiliation? she said. What are you talking about?

I was silent.

Finally she said: – You're crazy. I can't believe it. You're absolutely stark raving mad.

– You don't know these people, I said. You don't know the things they do.

– They're not doing anything, she said. They're letting you go.

I shook my head.

– All you have to do is get on that train with me, she said.

Suddenly she seemed to sense defeat. – You can't not come, she whispered.

– You don't know them as I do, I said.

– But you're free, she said. You can walk round the town now, can't you? You can eat where you want. You can come home at whatever hour you like. So why not just try getting on that train and see? If I'm wrong you'll learn soon enough.

– You don't know them, I said to her again. You don't know them like I do.

– You? she said, suddenly angry. What do you know about anything, stuck in this hole for years and years? You're the one who knows nothing. Absolutely nothing. And the fact of the

matter is that you don't want to go at all, do you? You're afraid
of leaving, afraid of facing the real world again, and you're even
afraid to admit that, so you dress it up as cynicism and hard-
won wisdom and pretend to be so much more aware of things
than other people. Well, as far as I'm concerned you can stay
here till the day you die.

How can you say goodbye to your sister, even a sister you
love very dearly, as the train puffs out of the station, when such
words have been exchanged? – Remember, she had said at the
end. Any time, if you change your mind, write and I'll send you
the money. But don't expect any loving letters from me after
this.

The funny thing is I did expect a letter or two from her, in
spite of what she'd said. I am still expecting them. But one learns
to expect in a different way here. One learns to live with such
expectations and one would be nonplussed to see them realised.
Sometimes, when I find myself near the station in my daily
perambulations through the town I go in and sit on one of the
benches facing the tracks and think back over her visit. Though
I had rather dreaded it in prospect, I must confess now that I
was glad to see her. Her face as she sat in my room imparting
her news, her eyes gleaming with pleasure and excitement,
hugging her knees – that is not a memory I will easily forget.
Indeed, it often slips into my mind at other moments of the
day, as I take my walks through the little town, for instance,
which I do every day, winter and summer. But never as I lie in
bed on those bitter-cold early mornings and stretch the blanket
taut between my feet.

# Steps

He had been living in Paris for many years.

Longer, he used to say, than he cared to remember.

When my first wife died, he would explain, there no longer seemed to be any reason to stay in England. So he moved to Paris and earned his living by translating.

He was an old-fashioned person, still put on a suit and tie to sit down to work, and a raincoat and hat when he went out. Even in the height of the Parisian summer he never went anywhere without his hat. At my age, he would say, I'm too old to change. Besides, I'm a creature of habit, always was.

He lived in a studio flat on the top of a peeling building in the rue Octave Mirbeau behind the Panthéon. To reach it you went through the narrow rue St. Julien and climbed a steep flight of steps on the right, which brought you out into the rue Octave Mirbeau opposite the building. There were other ways, of course, but this was the one he regularly used: it was how his flat joined on to the world outside.

From his desk, if he craned, he could just see the edge of the Panthéon. Every morning he was up at 6.00, had a look to see if the big monster was still there, made himself a light breakfast and was sitting down to work by 7.15. He kept at it till 11.15, when he put on his hat and coat and descended. He had a cup of coffee in a bar at the corner, did what little shopping was needed, ate a sandwich with a glass of beer at another nearby bar, and was back at his desk by 1.30. At 4.00 he knocked off for the day and made himself a pot of tea — he kept a supply of specially imported Ceylon tea in a wooden box with a red dragon stamped upon it, and was very precise about the amount of time he let it stand once the boiling water had been poured into the pot. Afterwards, if the weather was fine, he would take a stroll through the city. Sometimes this took him down as far as the river, or even the Louvre, at others he made straight for the Luxembourg Gardens and sat on a bench looking up into the trees. He was always back by 7.00, for that was the time a table was kept for him in a nearby bistro. He ate whatever was put in front of him and paid by the month without questioning the bill. After supper he would return to the flat and read a little or listen to music. He had a good collection of early music and his one indulgence was occasionally adding to it — Harnoncourt and the Concentus Musicus of Vienna he particularly admired.

— Sometimes you went to concerts, his wife — his second wife — would interrupt him. He seemed to need these inter-ruptions, was deft at incorporating them into his discourse. Not often, he would go on, too expensive and, really, after London, live music in Paris was nearly always a disappointment.

— We listen a lot here too, his wife would say. Friends who came to stay and neighbours who dropped in on them in their converted farmhouse in the Black Mountains, up above Abergavenny, were indeed often entertained to an evening of baroque music. His wife, a handsome woman still, with a mass of red hair piled high on her head, would hand the records to him reverently, dusting them as she did so with a special cloth. The final gestures – the laying of the disc on the turntable, the setting of the mechanism in motion, the gentle lowering of the stylus – she would leave to him. I'm so uneducated, she would say. When I met him I thought a saraband was something you wore round your head. You had other qualities, he would say.

In between records he would often talk about his Paris years. After his wife's death what he had needed most of all was solitude. Not that he wanted to meditate or brood; just that he didn't want to have to do with people. He took on more work than he could easily manage, needed to feel that when one piece was done there was always another waiting for him. Sometimes, in the spring or summer, in the early morning or evening, the light was excessively gentle, touching the teapot. I wouldn't ever have known moments like those if I hadn't been alone, he would say.

As he strolled through the city in the late afternoons he would occasionally have fantasies of drowning: a vivid sense of startled faces on the bank or the bridge above him, or perhaps on the deck of a passing boat at sea, and then the water would cover him completely, and he would sink, shedding parts of himself as he slowly descended into the silence and the dark, until in the end it was only a tiny core, a soul or knuckle perhaps, that lay, rocking gently with the current, on the sandy bottom. He knew such fantasies were neurotic, dangerous perhaps, but he was not unduly worried, sensed that it was better to indulge them, let them have their head, than to try and cut them out altogether. After all, everyone has fantasies. In the one life there are many lives. Different lives. Alternative lives. That's the fool-ishness of biographies, he would say, of novels. They never take account of the alternative lives we live alongside the main one.

In their converted farmhouse in the Black Mountains his wife would serve chilled white wine to anyone, friends or neighbours, who had dropped in to see them, always making sure that no glass was empty. You thought of alternative lives as you climbed the steps, she would say in her excellent English. You thought of alternative lives as you descended.

— Steps are conducive to fantasy, he would say. Going up and down steps lets the mind float free. How often we run up and down the steps of our lives, like scales on the piano.

— And always with his hat, his wife would say.

— Yes. Always with my hat. On my head. I'm a creature of habit. I would have felt naked without it.

And certainly she made life comfortable for him, saw to it that he had everything he needed, was not disturbed by any of the practical details of daily living. He for his part looked up to her, would do nothing without her consent, wanted her to say when he was tired and ready for bed, when he was hungry and ready for a meal.

He had been happy in his Paris flat. His desk was under the window and as he worked he felt the sun warm the top of his head and then his neck. If he gave his alternative lives their lead he also knew how to keep them in check. Most of the time I lived just one life, or less, he would say. When he poured tea into his cup in the early morning silence it sometimes seemed as if all of existence was concentrated in that one moment, that one act. Could he have wished for greater happiness?

But do you always know what it is you want? What it is you really feel? Sometimes the tediousness and unreality of the novels he had to translate was too much for him. It was an effort to keep going till 11.15, and then he couldn't bring himself to face the afternoon sessions. One day, indulging his drowning fantasies more than usual, he did not go back to his room after lunch. Instead, he walked down the hill and across the river to the Island, and then across again and up in the direction of the Bastille. He must have walked for two or three hours, his mind a blank, because he suddenly realised that he felt utterly exhausted, could not walk another step. There was a café across the road, so he crossed over and went in. It was empty at that time of day, except for the *patron* in his shirt-sleeves, polishing the counter. He eased himself on to a stool and ordered a coffee. When it came he swallowed it in one gulp and ordered another. This time he toyed with it a little longer, dipping a lump of sugar in it and watching the dark liquid eat into the white cube, letting it drop into the cup and stirring slowly, gazing down at the spoon as he did so.

By the time he had drunk this second cup he felt restored and wondered how he could have reached the state of exhaustion he had just been in.

— I want to make a phone call, he said to the *patron*.

The man stood in front of him, separated by the counter of the bar. He was a large man with a red face, bald but with a bristling moustache and large amounts of hair on his arms.

— Could I have a token please? For a phone call.

He thought the man had not heard, then saw that he was in fact holding out his hand, palm upward, and there lay the token on the creased red skin.

He looked into the man's face again. The man was grinning, holding his hand out across the polished counter. He lowered his eyes again and looked at the token. There it lay, waiting to be picked up. Gingerly, he stretched out his own hand and reached for it, but just as he was about to pick it up he realised it was no longer there. The large hand was open, palm upward, but it was empty.

He looked up quickly. The man was still grinning. He lowered his eyes again, and as he did so the man slowly turned his hand over, and there was the token again, a small silver circle, on the hairy back of the hand. The man thrust his arm forward as if to say, Go on, take it. So, once again, he watched his own hand going out to meet the other, and this time the fingers closed round the token and he lifted it off the hand and drew it back towards him. As he did so he saw the hole. It was a small round black hole in the middle of the man's hand, just where the token had been. It was smoking gently.

He must have walked a lot more after that. He didn't remember where or for how long, but towards the end of the afternoon he found himself by the river again. He tried to look at the books on sale on the quays, but his mind wouldn't focus. He didn't want to go back to the flat but his feet were hurting badly and he felt he had to take off his shoes or he would start to cry. He found some steps and staggered down to the level of the water. There was a patch of grass at the bottom, where a tree grew under the high wall. He sat down slowly, leaning back against the tree, closed his eyes, and fumbled with the laces of his shoes. When his feet were at last free he opened his eyes again and sat motionless, staring down into the water.

When the girl came it had grown almost dark. He couldn't make out her face clearly, only the mass of red hair that fell down to her shoulders under a little green beret. For a moment, in the half-light, she reminded him of his dead wife.

He must have spoken because she said at once:

– You are English.

– How did you guess?

– I guess.

He couldn't place her accent.

— It's hot today, she said. I will take off my shoes.

He wanted to talk about the token but checked himself.

She took off her shoes and then her beret. — Hold it please, she said.

She had produced a brush and was brushing her hair hard, moving her head in time to the strokes. Then the brush vanished as abruptly as it had appeared, and she took the beret back from him and carefully put it on, though this time at more of an angle than it had previously been.

He was looking at the lights of the city reflected in the river when she said to him: — Do you mind I put my head on your lap?

Without waiting for a reply she did so, quickly settling into position and tucking her legs under her skirt.

Her eyes were closed and he thought she had gone to sleep, but then she began to move her head on his lap, slowly at first, as though trying to find a more comfortable position, then with gathering violence. The beret fell off; he stroked her hair; she began to moan.

They must have got up together. He could remember nothing except that her room was red. Like fire, she said.

He found himself walking again, swaying like a drunkard. His trousers felt too tight, his thighs itched where they rubbed. His body seemed to have been scraped raw from neck to crotch. When he finally stumbled home he was so tired he could hardly get the key into the lock. He fell on the bed fully clothed and was asleep at once.

When he woke it was dark. He didn't know if he had slept for eight hours or thirty-two. To judge from his hunger it was probably the latter. He found some food in the fridge and wolfed it down. Then he got into his pyjamas and crawled into bed again.

The next time he woke it was early morning, He groped his way out of bed and to the window of the study for his daily look at the Panthéon. It was as he was doing so, craning a little to the left as usual, that he suddenly remembered that all had not been entirely normal in the past few days. Alternative lives, he thought to himself, made his breakfast and settled down to the novel on his desk.

It was only that evening, as he was having a shower, that he saw the wound in his thigh. It was a long straight cut, like a cat's scratch, and it ran all the way from the top of his thigh to his knee. He touched it but it didn't hurt. He dried it carefully, examined it again, and decided that there was nothing to do but let it heal and disappear. In fact, though, it never did. Years later, in Wales, whenever he talked of his Paris days he would point to his leg and laugh and say: It never healed.

— You didn't want it to, his wife would say. Friends who had known him in the old days would comment on the resemblance between his two wives. Especially when she stood in the middle of the room like that, dusting a record before handing it to him, saying: You didn't want it to, really. No, he would say, looking up at her. No I didn't, did I?

— He's so superstitious, she would say. He never went to a doctor about it.

— What could a doctor do?

— Maybe give you something to get rid of it.

— We've all got something like that somewhere on our bodies, he would say. Maybe if we got rid of it we wouldn't be ourselves any more, who knows?

— Who knows? his wife would echo.

He would tell of his fantasies of drowning, vivid images he experienced at that time, when he was living in Paris after the death of his first wife. As I sank I would feel quite relieved. I would think: There goes another life – and know I had not finished with this one.

– One sprouts many lives, he would say, and look at her and smile. One is a murderer. One an incendiary. One a suicide. One lives in London. One in Paris. One in New York.

– One, One, One, she would echo, mocking him.

With his soft grey hat pulled low over his eyes, he climbs the steps of the rue St. Julien.

# In the Fertile Land

We live in a fertile land. Here we have all we want. Beyond the borders, far away, lies the desert, where nothing grows.

Nothing grows there. Nor is there any sound except the wind.

Here, on the other hand, all is growth, abundance. The plants reach enormous heights, and even we ourselves grow and grow, so that there is absolutely no stopping us. And when we speak the words flow out in torrents, another aspect of the general fertility.

Here, the centre is everywhere and the circumference nowhere.

Conversely, it could be said – and it is an aspect of the general fertility here that everything that can be said has its converse side – conversely it could be said that the circumference is everywhere and the centre nowhere, that the limits are everywhere, that everywhere there is the presence of the desert.

Here, in the fertile land, everyone is so conscious of the desert, so intrigued and baffled by it, that a law has had to be passed forbidding anyone to mention the word.

Even so, it underlies every sentence and every thought, every dream and every gesture.

Some have even gone over into the desert, but as they have not come back it is impossible to say what they found there.

I myself have no desire to go into the desert. I am content with the happy fertility of this land. The desert beyond is not something I think about very much, and if I occasionally dream about it, that contravenes no law. I cannot imagine where the limits of the desert are to be found or what kind of life, if any, exists there. When I hear the wind I try to follow it in my mind across the empty spaces, to see in my mind's eye the ripples it makes in the enormous dunes as it picks up the grains of sand and deposits them in slightly altered patterns a little further along – though near and far have clearly quite different meanings in the desert from the one they have here.

In the desert silence prevails. Here the talk is continuous. Many of us are happy even talking to ourselves. There is never any shortage of subjects about which to talk, nor any lack of words with which to talk. Sometimes, indeed, this abundance becomes a little onerous, the sound of all these voices raised in animated conversation or impassioned monologue grows slightly disturbing. There have even been moments when the very abundance of possible subjects and of available directions in which any subject may be developed has made me long for the silence of the desert, with only the monotonous whistling of the wind for sound. At those times my talk redoubles in both quantity and speed and I cover every subject except the one that obsesses me – for the penalty for any infringement of the law is severe. Even as I talk, though, the thought strikes me that perhaps I am actually in the desert already, that I have crossed over and not returned, and that what the desert is really like is this, a place where everyone talks but where no one speaks of what concerns him most.

Such thoughts are typical of the fertility of our land.

# The Plot Against the Giant

The summons went out at noon. We assembled under 'the daisy'. In every kitchen pages of 'the manual' peeled from the walls. Upon inspection it was found that our 'equipment' was in order and that we were ready for 'action'. Well-trained, well-equipped, well-led, we were aching for 'the big day'.

We marched 'by company', in single file, through the 'forest', always keeping close to the base of the 'mountain', and converging at last on the 'clearing' where the giant lay sleeping.

Without a word, for we all knew what had to be done, we deployed our 'ropes' and 'pegs'. One company was assigned 'the head', another 'the shoulders', and so on down. Ours was assigned the left foot and ankle. The giant breathed deeply and steadily, his chest rising and falling like a mountain high above us. The air, as we set to, was heavy with his breath.

The work proceeded apace. Some of us were 'detached' and ordered to climb onto his chest, hauling up 'the ropes', and then to throw them down to those waiting on the other side; some to light fires in order to weld the 'manacles'; some to sharpen the 'pegs'; some to man the 'field-kitchen'.

We worked for as long as it took. There was no question of rest or respite. As soon as it was done we 're-formed', and 'presented arms'. A great feeling of relief spread through us. No longer in thrall to the giant, no longer driven by unassuageable desires, impossible dreams and fantasies, we would at last be free to be ourselves. Already the celebrations were being planned. The 'mothers' hung out the bunting, while the 'carpenters' made the 'wheels'. In the trees 'lanterns' lay hidden, waiting for the world to come to life. In the municipal kitchens the 'fowl' were being prepared for roasting, the 'fish' for frying, and, out of the cellars where they had, throughout the years of our servitude, been kept cool, the 'puddings' were being taken.

But then, abruptly, the giant cleared his throat. He ceased to breathe his deep regular breaths. The air grew quiet. All of us still working on him were immediately ordered off. He opened wide his eyes and tried to move, but found that he could not. Our hearts were in our mouths. The giant turned his head to one side and then to the other. We who were on his left side saw his left eye, open wide, considering us. Then, very slowly, he stood up, shaking off his shackles. And a huge feeling of relief flooded through us, as though we had all of us been waiting for him to do just that, as though the plot against him and its execution had been nothing but a charade, a ritual to which we no longer had the key. There we were again, 'in thrall' to the giant, and our relief, I would even say our happiness, was palpable to all.

# A Modern Fairy Tale

Once upon a time there was a little boy who lived in a land of reeds. Wherever you went the great river or one of its tributaries was always close at hand. But though the river, which had its source far away in the Mountains of the West, had almost reached its destination in the vast inland sea as it passed through the land of reeds, the land was so flat and so interspersed with streams that few of those who lived there had ever seen the sea.

The little boy lived in a big house with his father and mother and many servants, for his father was one of the richest men in the land. He had grown rich by bringing the railway to the land of reeds, and every year the family would pack their bags and board one of the trains for which his father had been responsible and travel in great luxury to the big city which had once been the capital of an empire. There they would stay in a splendid hotel and his father would take him to concerts and to cafés and to see the horses in the famous riding school. Once men went on pilgrimages to holy shrines, his father would say, now they go on pilgrimages to the shrine of Culture.

The little boy had a nurse from the village, whom he loved, and a tutor from the big city, whom he hated. The tutor was there to teach him history and geography and the language of the city, and no one in the big house was allowed to speak the language of the grandparents or the language of the village, though the nurse whispered it to him on their walks along the river banks. You must grow up speaking the true language of Civilisation, his father told him. That is the language of the great poets and you must never forget that it is the culture of the great poets to which you belong.

But one day the visits to the great city stopped. Uncle, father's brother, came to stay, and the little boy could hear him and his father shouting in the library and sometimes his mother shut herself up in her room for the whole day and when she came down he could see that she had been crying. Then Uncle went away and shortly after that men in uniform, speaking the language of the great poets, came and took them away. Though the little boy clung to his mother she ran back into the house and the men shouted and there was a loud noise and then they put him and his father in a car and drove them away. They were men in a hurry. They drove the little boy and his father to the station and put them in a train that was waiting. This was not at all a luxury train such as the one they took when they went to the big city, but a train crowded with people who spoke the language of the grandparents. Where are we going? the little boy asked. Where is Mother? But all his father would say was: I cannot believe it, I cannot believe it.

After a long journey the little boy and his father were taken from the train with all the other people crowded in there and pushed into a courtyard. Everybody was crying and the men in uniform were shouting orders which nobody understood and hitting people with their guns. But after a while life settled down to a routine. It was very different from life in the big house.

Everybody slept together in one huge room which smelt so bad you wanted to be sick. The only food was a thin soup and occasionally a small piece of stale bread. The men in uniform shouted the whole time and beat the people. Every morning before the sun was up everybody had to get up and dress and go down in long rows to the quarry. You did not get back from the quarry till the sun had set. Your hands and back hurt so much from the quarry that you could not sleep, and people cried in the dark and cursed in the language of the grandparents.

The little boy decided to escape. He stepped out of the line as they were going down to the quarry and hid behind a tree. Then, when the guards had passed and no one seemed to have noticed, he began to run. He ran for a long time, his heart pounding in his chest and the taste of blood in his mouth, but no one shouted and no one came after him. Night fell and he stumbled and hurt his leg. So he crawled under a bush and went to sleep.

The next day it was raining. The little boy ate some berries from a tree and went on walking as fast as he could. His only thought was to keep moving. Once he came within sight of a village, but although he was hungry he skirted round it, keeping to the forest, and went on walking. That night he slept in the forest, covering himself with leaves, but the next morning he had terrible pains in his stomach and he found it almost impossible to get up. He knew he would have to get food that day even if it meant having to talk to people. And, soon enough, he heard the sound of farm animals and of people at work in the fields. He heard them shouting to each other and he remembered the language of the village he had been forbidden to speak and knew he would have to speak it now or his life would be over.

When he reached the village – it was no more than a poor

collection of houses and huts lining a dirt track – his heart was pounding. But he felt so weak he knew there was no alternative. He knocked at a door and when an old woman opened he asked her, in the language his nurse had whispered to him as they walked along the river banks, whether she might have a crust of bread for him. He did not understand the stream of words that issued from her mouth but stood, looking at her, until her face grew blurred and he felt himself falling.

He did not entirely lose consciousness but he kept his eyes shut tight as the voices rose and fell around him and many hands picked him up and laid him on a couch. Then he opened his eyes and saw them all looking at him and said again, in the language of his nurse, Bread, bread. The old woman who had opened the door brought him bread and milk and the others watched as he ate. They asked him questions but an instinct told him not to answer even those he could understand. So he closed his eyes again and fell into a heavy sleep.

When he woke up he did not at first know where he was. He thought he was in his room in the big house and then all the events of the past few months came rushing back into his mind and he grew very still. He listened but there was not a sound in the house. He got up and found that he was still dressed, though someone had taken off his shoes and put them at the foot of the couch. He put them on, listening out for any noises, but the house was silent. He went to the door and listened again, then opened it and found himself in a hall with another door in front of him. He opened that and peered out into the street, but the village seemed to be deserted. Even the old woman must be down in the fields, he thought. He ran quickly along the track and soon found himself in the forest again.

After that he planned more carefully. He went into the villages to beg for food and went back into the forest as soon as he could. He knew that one point in his favour was that he looked more like the village children than like the other children with whom he had been shut up in the camp. His face was round, his skin blackened by the days in the quarry, his eyes twinkling. If I don't talk much I may be able to get away with it, he thought.

— How terrible it must have been, someone would usually say at this point when, years later, a famous author now, and living in another country, speaking another language, he would tell audiences round the world about his childhood. — How dreadful to be a child alone in those forests with your life threatened at any moment.

— You know, he would say, the twinkle still bright in his eye, it was not terrible. Perhaps to think about it is terrible, but when you are living something then you are just living it. And when you are a child it is perhaps easier. You do not think too much. You live one day and then you live another day. You are not anxious about the day after that.

— But how did you survive? he would be asked.

— I survived, he would say. For three years. Maybe four. And then I was found by the other army and I travelled with them. It was with them I learned to smoke, he would say, laughing. From the age of twelve I was smoking cigarettes. That is not good for the health, but when you are young you do not know any better. Last year I was in hospital for my chest and I had to stop.

— And you wandered like that, all that time? he would be asked.

— You know, he would say, his eyes twinkling, when you

are small you do not want to go to school. You do not want to sit in a classroom and read books all day long. You want to be free and to be out in the woods and the fields. And that is what happened to me. I had the best education anybody could have, he would say. The people I met on my travels, they were the people on the margins of the villages, the gypsies, the horse-thieves, the prostitutes, the very old mad people in the villages of the forests. They gave me food, sometimes clothes, and they told wonderful stories. Wonderful stories. What more could a child want? And then, when I was old and I wanted to study, he would say, I was able to go to university and listen to the very greatest, to many famous names who had come to the new country and wished to be of service to it. What better education could there be?

— If I was Minister of Education, he would say, his eyes bright, then I would insist that everybody should have the education that I had. But how would that be possible now?

— And what happened after the other army found you? someone would ask.

— You know, he would say, after many months I got to the south, to the land of the sun. There was a group of us. A priest took us in. He was sorry for us and he took us in and fed us and looked after us. He taught us how to say prayers. He wanted us to become priests too and we didn't know any better, we liked him, we were willing to do as he said. And then one day a man came and he called us together and he explained to us who and what we were. So we left the priest and went with this man and waited on the beaches for a boat to come and take us to the new country. We waited for a long time but in the end a boat came and we were taken on board.

That was the time they were attacking those boats, he said,

to stop them getting to their destination. But I got there. Some of my friends did not get there, they were drowned in the boats that were sunk, but I was fortunate and I got there.

— After I had been in the new country for a year, he said, I suddenly could not do anything any more and I could not speak to people any more. I looked at my hands and I did not know they were my hands. I looked at my face in the mirror and I could not understand how it was my face. But then slowly I recovered and I began to be able to speak to the people around me and to do the things I had to do. When I looked at my hands they were still strange to me but I knew that they were mine.

— After that, he said, I went to school and learned the language of the new country and then I went to the university and after that I got married and had my children. Of course there were the wars, he said. I fought in three wars. In the first, after ten days of learning how to fire a rifle, we were told we would have to take back a bare hill that the enemy had captured. If you left the cover of the trees and started to climb the hill you were completely exposed, and they had machine guns up there, we knew that because they were our machine guns which they had captured. So we knew that once we left the cover of the trees and started up the hill it was only a matter of minutes before our lives would end. But we were soldiers and we had to obey orders. If someone thought it would help for us to be killed like that then we had to be killed. That is the logic of war. But fortunately, he said, just before the order to advance was given another message came from headquarters and we were told to retreat instead. So again I survived.

After a little while, as he seemed disinclined to continue, someone said: — May I ask whether you ever heard what happened to your father?

— Every week, he said, from the time I arrived, I looked in the papers where they have a list of people who have arrived in the country. I did not expect to see his name but I looked. Every week. Like a ritual. And one day I was looking and I saw his name. The names were printed very small and all close together because so many people were arriving in those days, so my eye went past it, but my brain told me to stop. I went back slowly over the list and there was his name. There are not many with our name, he said, but it was quite possible of course that it was not him. I made enquiries and they told me where this person with his name had been sent on his arrival. So I went and I asked and they looked at the list and then at another list, and they said, He is in the orchard. So I went to the orchard, there were many trees and in each tree there was a man, up in the branches, picking the fruit. So I went from tree to tree looking up to see if I recognised the man up there. And finally I came to a tree and I looked and there was my father.

In the silence that followed someone said: — It's really like a fairy tale, your life.

— You see, he said, and his eyes twinkled more than ever, it is a fairy tale, but it is a modern fairy tale. Why? For two reasons. One is that my own life has been like a fairy tale, but I cannot forget that my mother disappeared. She disappeared, and many others with her. If this was a traditional fairy tale, he said, this would not have happened, and then if perhaps it had happened I would have no memory of it. But I will always have the memory. I cannot forget it. So it is a fairy tale but it is a modern fairy tale.

— The other reason, he said, is that the new country, in which I live and whose language I speak and in whose language I write, and where by the grace of God I have become a well-known writer, so that I am invited here to talk to you and my good friend the cultural attaché looks after me and brings me here and my other good friends make me welcome in their beautiful flat and you are invited here to listen to me – this country too is like a fairy tale. Fifty years ago it did not exist and now there are cities and orchards and schools and universities and printing presses and here children can be brought up in safety and happiness and in their turn bring up their children. It is a miracle, it is a fairy tale. But it too is a modern fairy tale. Because here too there is something we cannot forget. We cannot forget that before we came this land was not empty. We cannot forget that there were people here with houses and villages and their own language and their own stories and their own memories. And if we wanted to forget they would not let us forget, for they cannot forget that they have lost fields and houses and fathers and husbands and sons. I do not say it is our fault. I do not say they are blameless. I only say they cannot forget and they will not let us forget. So it is a fairy tale but it is a modern fairy tale.

– You see, he said, we must never forget that fairy tales can occur, even in our modern world. For if we forget this then we will cease to be human beings. But we must also never forget that all fairy tales exist in a context which is not that of fairy tales, a context of pain and loss and failure and death. There will always be fairy tales as long as there are human beings, he said, but we must never forget that all fairy tales exist in a context which is not that of fairy tales. And now I see that food and drink have been prepared by our kind hostess, so let us eat and refresh ourselves, so that tomorrow we may be ready to go out and face another day.

# Donne Undone

All who saw him climb unsteadily into the pulpit knew at once that the end they had so long feared had come at last. 'Many of them thought', wrote a contemporary, 'he presented himself not to preach mortification by a living voice, but mortality by a decayed body and a dying face.'

The text he had chosen for this sermon, delivered at Whitehall before the King himself in the beginning of Lent (25 February) 1631, was taken from Psalm 68: 'And unto God the Lord belong the issues of death.' 'Many that then saw his tears and heard his faint and hollow voice', the chronicler continues, 'professed they thought the text prophetically chosen, and that the Dean had preached his own funeral sermon.'

Having gathered himself together for the effort (he had refused to comply with the fervent wishes of his doctor and his friends that he cancel the engagement), he found, after a few uncertain seconds, that the power of his voice was barely diminished by his recent illness, and that the old excitement of performing – on whatever stage, but pre-eminently on this one – had quite driven away any doubts he might secretly have entertained as to his ability to accomplish this, his final public duty.

He had always liked to start strongly, both in the poetry he had once written and in the sermons that had by now taken its place. If the foundations are securely laid then the building, no matter how elaborate and fanciful, will give little trouble — that had always been his principle, and he had been fortunate in having a gift for the strong opening. Today was no exception. Indeed, the first image was precisely that of a building and what keeps it from falling down:

> Buildings stand by the benefit of their foundations, that sustain and support them, and of their buttresses that comprehend and embrace them, and of their contignations that knit and unite them. The foundations suffer them not to sink, the buttresses suffer them not to swerve, and the contignation and knitting suffers them not to cleave.

And now for the application:

> The body of our building is in the former part of this verse. It is this: He that is our God is the God of salvation: *ad salutes*, of salvations in the plural, so it is in the original; the God that gives...

He found it difficult to make out his congregation as anything more than a blur. Too much reading had caught up with him, that hydroptic thirst for knowledge to which he had confessed though he had always been able to do without spectacles. But he felt their presence, felt their extreme attention — he had always been acutely aware of his audience, that had been one of the reasons for his success as a preacher, whether in the open air of Paul's Cross or in the great echoing spaces of the

Cathedral, in the humble parish church of St. Dunstan's or here
before the King at Whitehall.

> For first the foundation of this building (that our God is
> the God of all salvations) is laid in this: That unto this God
> the Lord belong the issues of death, that is, it is in his power
> to give us an issue and deliverance, even then when we are
> brought to the jaws and teeth of death, and to the lips of
> that whirlpool, the grave...

That death was the mouth of the old enemy was a common-
place, but even in his present condition he felt the old familiar
thrill of pleasure at the way he had brought the period to its
close, moving rapidly from the key word, *lips*, to *whirlpool* and
then to *grave*. That had always been his mark, this ability to
change direction at speed, barely giving the reader or listener
time to adjust to a new focus before altering it again. As he
threw the sentence out into the great hall he rejoiced once again
at the way he had found to flesh out the common tropes before
consigning them, with a single final pause after *whirlpool*, to
oblivion, by ending with that most ordinary word, now made
new and startling by the fantasies that had preceded it — *the grave*.

Not much longer though. This time he had known at once
that there would be no escape. Of course there had been alarms
before, in his great sickness eight years earlier, or that other,
many years previously, in Mitcham. But the attacks then had
been sudden, violent, as though a force had seized him from
without and immediately rendered him powerless. This time
though it had come upon him slowly, and from within, helped
on by another bout of fever and then by the death of his beloved
mother in her eightieth year, not five weeks since. That had

finally sapped what little strength remained to him, and without further ado he had made his will and sat down to compose this sermon. He had written it out carefully, afraid of the tricks his phenomenal and well-trained memory might play upon him, afraid of the effort it would cost him to learn it by rote.

As he delivered the text now, glancing up occasionally to see how the King, in his raised chair facing him across the hall, was taking it, but unable to make out his features at that distance, his mind, always liable to wander when he was well launched on a sermon, flickered this way and that before settling on the thought that had struck him so forcibly while he was preparing the sermon and making sketches for his monument, that sermon in stone whose place in the Cathedral he had already reserved.

Unto God the Lord belong the issues of death, that is, the disposition and manner of our death: what kind of issue and transmigration we shall have out of this world, whether prepared or sudden, whether violent or natural, whether in our perfect senses or shaken and disordered by sickness...

The thought was this: Why, even at such a time as this, do I still so much enjoy the idea of acting out a role? Why am I so thrilled, even now, by the thought of standing up in the pulpit, a man so obviously dying, and preaching to them about death? Why does my heart beat faster at the thought of sitting for my last portrait clothed in nothing but a shroud? Is it not time to put aside these childish things and to compose myself in the right spirit of humility for what must come?

First, then, we consider this *exitus mortis*, to be *liberatio a morte*,

that with God the Lord are the issues of death, and there-
fore in all our deaths, and deadly calamities of this life, we
may justly hope of a good issue from him...

He had always felt a little uneasy with this propensity of his for
play-acting. And yet, at the same time, when it came to it, he
had never been able to resist the impulse, had felt, indeed, that
he only came alive when he threw himself into the part of the
cynic, the wounded lover, the humble petitioner, the husband,
the father, the penitent, the preacher...

But then this *exitus a morte* is but *introitus in mortem*, this issue,
this deliverance from that death, the death of the womb, is
an entrance, a delivering over to another death, the mani-
fold deaths of this world...

Had not God put us on earth for a purpose, he wondered,
hearing his voice echoing round the great hall, had He not made
us in His image for a reason? If this was how God had made
him would it not have been sinful to deny it? And he felt again
in his guts his old anger at the Jesuits for trying to force
martyrdom on those born in the Catholic faith. His uncle had
been made to suffer imprisonment and exile for the cause. And
were they not responsible for his brother's death, as they had
been responsible for so many needless deaths? Either an apos-
tate or a martyr, they had insisted. But the choice was a false
one. He had refused to submit to their blackmail. Even though
(as his mother never tired of reminding him) he was a descen-
dant of the greatest English Catholic martyr of them all, Sir
Thomas More. More More More. Always more. She had never
let him forget. But he had held out. Had escaped the Jesuit

clutches. Had made his way alone, determined to live out to the full the life God had blessed him with. As He would surely have wanted him to. For what use to God was a brain like his, a spirit like this, if he was to be hanged and disembowelled before he had had a chance to put those gifts to use?

And yet what had he done with them? Read a great many books. Written a little poetry. Fallen in love rather too often. Made many friends. Seen service as a soldier. Travelled. Married. Become a father to umpteen children. Become a priest. And then a widower. And all his life, it seemed, since he had made that conscious decision to reject the false Jesuit alternative, all his life he had been searching for something solid, for firm ground under his feet, that would enable him to jump up and seize his rightful reward, to rise up and become fully himself. But instead everything slipped from his grasp, crumbled in his hands as soon as he grasped it. Was it for this then that he had denied the faith into which he was born? Was it for this he had refused the martyrdom that had been his for the taking? *Here*, he heard himself saying to the assembled congregation,

> here we have no continuing city, nay no cottage that continues, nay no persons, no bodies, that continue... Even the Israel of God hath no mansions, but journeys, pilgrimages in this life...

Why had God done this to him? Why had he filled him with this immoderate thirst for knowledge, for experience, if it was only to thwart him at every turn? And his anger, as he pitched his voice to the furthest reaches of the enormous chamber, turned once more against God. Not against his mother, not against his brother, not against the Jesuits — but against God, who had put him in this impossible position, filled him with these contrary desires. *That which we call life*, he heard his voice proceeding, and he had been in the pulpit long enough to know instinctively how to give the words just the right inflexion, just the right weight, though his mind, by then, was far away:

> That which we call life is but *hebdomada mortium*, a week of deaths, seven periods of our life spent in dying, a dying seven times over; and there is an end. Our birth dies in infancy, and our infancy dies in youth, and youth and the rest die in age, and age also dies, and determines all...

He had sought for employment that would ground him solidly in the world, but it was not forthcoming. He recalled the many letters he had written from Mitcham: 'I would fain be or do something: but, that I cannot tell what, it is no wonder...; for to choose is to do; but to be no part of any body, is to be as nothing; and so I am, and shall so judge my self, unless I could be so incorporated into a part of the world, as by business to contribute some sustentation to the whole.' But nothing had come of such letters.

He had dreamed of a perfect union which would at least provide a focus for his many desires, and he had even celebrated it in verse:

> Twice or thrice had I loved thee,
> Before I knew thy face or name;
> So in a voice, so in a shapeless flame,
> Angels affect us oft, and worshipped be;
>     Still when, to where thou wert, I came,

Some lovely glorious nothing did I see,
    But since my soul, whose child love is,
Takes limbs of flesh, and else could nothing do,
    More subtle than the parent is
Love must not be, but take a body too,
    And therefore what thou wert, and who
        I bid love ask, and now
That it assume thy body, I allow
And fix itself in thy lip, eye, and brow.

He had always despised the idealism of the sonneteers, known that his dream of a union not just of spirits but of bodies too was infinitely more interesting, more satisfying, than the abstract love they celebrated. Besides, his dreams had always come clothed in flesh, and flesh, he knew, was the home of the spirit:

As our blood labours to beget
    Spirits as like souls as it can,
Because such fingers need to knit
    That subtle knot, which makes us man:
So must pure lovers' souls descend
    T'affections, and to faculties,
Which sense may reach and apprehend,
    Else a great prince in prison lies...

And then one day he found her. Another More. Anne More. He had married her, thirteen years his junior, still a minor, and so had risked prison for her, as if to prove to himself that here at last he had found something truly worth suffering for. But nothing had changed. His life had not been transformed, except in so far as he had found his prospects in the world destroyed for ever. So they had retired to the damp cottage in Mitcham and she had given birth to child after child, as God had willed. But still his all-consuming thirst was unassuaged. The new situation merely made time pass more slowly and exacerbated his sense that more was due to him than he was receiving, that life, his life, the only life God had given him, could not simply be this, a loving wife and a damp cottage far from the centre and the feeling that time was passing and he had nothing to show for it.

He had been stricken by her death. It had forced one of his finest poems out of him, that 'Nocturnal Upon S. Lucie's Day' which he would still exchange for almost any other of his poems:

'Tis the year's midnight, and it is the day's,
Lucy's, who scarce seven hours herself unmasks.
  The sun is spent, and now his flasks
  Send forth light squibs, no constant rays;
    The world's whole sap is sunk:
The general balm th'hydroptic earth hath drunk,
Whither, as to the bed's feet, life is shrunk,
Dead and interred; yet all these seem to laugh,
Compared with me, who am their epitaph.

Perhaps its quality derived from the pain that had forced it out of him. At the same time there was no denying the pleasure that had spread like a gentle flame through his body as the image of the bed's feet came to him. It did not drive away the pain but co-existed with it.

But for us that die now and sleep in the state of the dead, we must all pass this posthume death, this death after death, nay this death after burial, this dissolution after dissolution, this death of corruption and putrefaction and vermicula-tion and incineration, of dissolution and dispersion in and from the grave, when these bodies that have been the chil-dren of royal parents, and the parents of royal children, must say with Job, Corruption thou art my father, and to the worm, thou art my mother and my sister. Miserable riddle, when the same worm must be my mother, and my sister and myself. Miserable incest, when I must be married to my mother and my sister, and be both father and mother to my own mother and sister: when my mouth shall be filled with dust, and the worm shall feed sweetly upon me...

There it was again, that lingering on dissolution, disintegration, annihilation. *Absence, darkness, death; things which are not,* as he had put it in the Nocturnal. Was it sheer morbidity on his part? And why did his spirit quicken at that 'sweetly' which had not quickened at the mention of the resurrection itself?

He is, he realises, in particularly good voice today; his words are ringing out powerfully and he can sense his audience straining forward in their seats, caught once more as he has so often caught them in the past.

He had married a More and found that he could never have done with Donne. And it was if the more he pleaded with God, argued with Him, threatened Him even, to remove that burden from him, the heavier it grew. For even the pleas and threats seemed to become a kind of game, a kind of play-acting, under his hand:

Batter my heart, three-personed God; for you
As yet but knock, breathe, shine, and seek to mend;
That I may rise, and stand, o'erthrow me, and bend
Your force, to break, blow, burn, and make me new.
. . .
　　dearly I love you, and would be loved fain,
But am betrothed unto your enemy:
Divorce me, untie, or break that knot again,
Take me to you, imprison me, for I
Except you enthral me, never shall be free,
Nor ever chaste, except you ravish me.

Curious pleasure those lines had given him. As if even the asser-
tion of his desperate state were itself one more proof of his
betrothal to the enemy. Was this then what he had refused
martyrdom for, the old serpent's first last trick? *That monarch*, he
read from his text, and looked straight across to where he knew
the King to be, on his raised seat above the throng,

That monarch, who spread over many nations alive, must
in his dust lie in a corner of that sheet of lead, and there,
but so long as that lead will last, and that private and retired
man, that thought himself his own for ever, and never came
forth, must in his dust of the grave be published, and (such
are the revolutions of the graves) be mingled with the dust
of every highway, and of every dunghill and swallowed in
every puddle and pond: this is the most inglorious and
contemptible nullification of man, that we can consider. . .

'O think me worth thine anger, punish me,' he had entreated
God in that Good Friday poem, written as he rode from

Polesworth to Montgomery Castle. 'Burn off my rusts and my deformities', return me, in other words, to my first self, to what I was before Adam's transgression and fall, when I was made in Your image and nothing had yet happened to tarnish that image. For from that time on we are condemned to wander far from the truth, encrusted with that which is not ourselves, lost in a labyrinth of games. Games. Always games. Even here, at the end of this poem of entreaty, he had found himself playing games with God: 'Restore thine image, so much, by thy grace, That thou mayest know me, and I'll turn my face.' If you remove Adam's sin from me, restore me to that self in which you first made me, then, and only then, will I turn to you. Be able to turn. Be inclined to turn. The poem had led him into that challenge. The words themselves had, as always, taken over. Not that he did not stand by them. As he wrote he felt the pleasure of the ambiguity. But all that showed was that he was still clothed in corruption, still incapable of feeling what he ought to feel, of speaking as he ought to speak – and how then could he expect God to listen?

And so it had always been. Even in his great sickness, after his wife's death, after ten years in the habit of a priest. Even then he had found that his way of talking to God was itself the sign of his distance from Him. For this way of talking did indeed give him a deep and perverse pleasure, even as he recognised that pleasure as the sign of his damnation. That had been the poem in which he had tried to sum up his life, the poem in which More and Donne had played hide-and-seek through the lines and he had, while composing it, quite forgotten what he had set out to do, so engrossed had he become in the actual doing:

Wilt thou forgive that sin where I begun,
    Which is my sin, though it were done before?
Wilt thou forgive those sins, through which I run,
    And do run still: though still I do deplore?
        When thou hast done, thou hast not done,
        For I have more.

Wilt thou forgive that sin by which I have won
    Others to sin? and made my sin their door?
Wilt thou forgive that sin which I did shun
    A year, or two: but wallowed in, a score?
        When thou hast done, thou hast not done,
        For I have more.

I have a sin of fear, that when I have spun
    My last thread, I shall perish on the shore:
Swear by thy self, that at my death thy son
    Shall shine as he shines now, and heretofore;
        And, having done that, Thou hast done,
        I fear no more.

But, as so often, the last verse was much less convincing than
the others. For what, after all, did it say? Only that *if* God swore,
then he would fear no more. But there was no guarantee that
He would ever do so – indeed, He had not talked to men since
the days of the Prophets. So, even after the poem was finished,
God had not Donne, only Donne had Donne – more and more
Donne. More and more. And there would always be more.
There was no end to it.

    He became aware that there was a shuffling and a rustling
in the assembled congregation. He had stopped speaking as he

recalled the poem and its circumstances, and faces were looking up at him, wondering at his silence. Hurriedly he found his place and pressed on:

> This death of incineration and dispersion is, to natural reason, the most irrecoverable death of all, and yet, *Domini Domini sunt exitus mortis,* unto God the Lord belong the issues of death, and by recompacting this dust into the same body, and reinanimating the same body with the same soul, He shall in a blessed and glorious resurrection give me such an issue from this death, as shall never pass into any other death, but establish me into a life that shall last as long as the Lord of life himself...

Now there was a sigh from those below him. This was the fulcrum of the sermon, this was what they had come to hear. He had paused at precisely the right place, as though even in his distraction his old dramatic instinct had been in control.

But what did the words mean? What did he mean by the words?

He hurried on:

> The tree lies as it falls it's true, but it is not the last stroke that fells the tree, nor the last word nor gasp that qualifies the soul. Our critical day is not the very day of our death; but the whole course of our life. I thank him that prays for me when the bell tolls, but I thank him much more that catechises me, or preaches to me, or instructs me how to live...

A didactic point, a preacherly point, but perhaps it meant more than he had understood it to mean when he penned the lines. Our critical day is not the very day of our death but the whole course of our life, that was what he was beginning, but just beginning, to understand. He had always written about sudden change, about moments of total transformation, and when the poem was over nothing at all was changed. But perhaps he had misunderstood himself. Perhaps there were no sudden changes. Perhaps there is no critical moment — but the whole course of our life. 'I wonder by my troth what thou and I/ Did, till we loved?' he had written.

> Were we not weaned till then,
> But sucked on country pleasures, childishly?
> Or snorted we in the seven sleepers' den?
> 'Twas so; but this, all pleasures fancies be,
> If ever any beauty I did see,
> Which I desired, and got, 'twas but a dream of thee.

But we are never weaned, we go on snorting in the seven sleepers' den for the whole of our lives. All beauty is but a dream of beauty. That is what life is, he thought. That is what beauty is. There is no life of wakefulness elsewhere, no true beauty round the corner. And that is as it should be.

His mind was suddenly alive with his earlier verse:

> Busy old fool, unruly sun,
> Why dost thou thus,
> Through windows, and through curtains call on us?
> Must to thy motions lovers' seasons run?
> Saucy pedantic wretch, go chide
> Late school-boys, and sour prentices,

> Go tell court-huntsmen, that the King will ride
>     Call country ants to harvest offices;
> Love, all alike, no season knows, nor clime,
> Nor hours, days, months, which are the rags of time.

What had filled him with pleasure had been his ability to assert the triumphant escape from time even as he marked its work in the very rhythm and pace of the verse. No one had done that before him, not Dante, not Spenser, not Shakespeare or Jonson. The rags of time. Ah yes. He had found a way to do it, or perhaps it would be truer to say that he had been forced to discover a way by the path of frustration, the constant and debilitating sense of time passing. 'Grief brought to numbers cannot be so fierce,/ For he tames it that fetters it in verse', he had written in another poem, and that, in the end, was what it all came down to. Though perhaps the grief remained equally fierce, but alongside it an equally fierce joy was fanned into life.

But it was more complicated even than that. Fettering grief in his time-bound, earth-bound verse had the effect, paradoxically, of releasing him. Without these fetters a great prince – his essential self – in prison lay. Yet, fettered, he rose up, a new Samson, no, not a destroyer like Samson but a new, yes, a new Adam.

It was as if a huge and diffuse weight, which had been crushing him all his life had suddenly been lifted from him. He saw with great clarity that poetry was not of the devil but of God. Our critical day is not the day of our death but the whole course of our life. Truth is not on the further side of language but in language itself. This was God, life, the resurrection even. His error had been to look for that which would be stable, which would lie outside time, change, the ageing of the body and the vagaries of language. He had looked for it in women, in God, in the Church. But there was no stability. There was only life. He had wanted to have done with confusion, uncertainty, the horrors of waste and change. And the more he had wanted it the less he had found it, His Anne, Anne More, had known better, as she bore him child after child. But he had been blind to it. God is not outside the world, aloof, disdainful, cunning and deceitful. He is in the ever-changing fabric of the world. And so language, and poetry, are not an aberration, an instrument of the old enemy, but the very form of the godhead. And this, he thought, my poetry has in fact always known. My poetry but not me. It has taken me a lifetime to find it out.

Somewhere at the back of his mind, as he went on speaking to the assembled court – he thought he saw the King nodding in sleep now he had turned the corner of the sermon and come to the glorious resurrection – somewhere at the back of his mind, as his voice faltered and then found a new strength (he felt the thickness of the remaining pages of his sermon between the thumb and forefinger of his right hand and realised with a mixture of sadness and relief that he had come almost to the end of his last public performance) – somewhere at the back of his mind words were forming. They had to do with green leaves covering a rock, covering a high rock... He knew the words were not his and would never be his, yet they hovered in his mind as though one day he would speak them. All his life, he now saw, he had looked for the rock, and never realised that there is no rock but only leaves, frail, fallible, constantly in motion, falling and returning, but outlasting the rock, more real than the rock. These leaves are the poem, he thought, they are ourselves and the world too.

Later, as he lay dying, the picture of himself in his shroud

on the wall before him, the words echoed in his mind and he
knew that his violent and unnatural thirst had been the result
not of a lack but of a gift. Now his boat was setting out. It was
a boat made of stones yet it sailed on, with him at the prow,
leaning and looking before him like someone familiar with what
was happening, familiar with the point of arrival, a long-term
denizen of those waters, which were different from the waters
he had sailed on, from any waters ever known, and yet were
familiar, so that he entered them as one enters a long-inhabited
house, eats from a familar bowl.

Or, as a contemporary put it: 'Being speechless, and seeing
heaven by that illumination by which he saw it; he did as St.
Stephen, look steadfastly into it, till he saw the Son of Man,
standing at the right hand of God his father; and being satis-
fied with this blessed sight, as his soul ascended and his last
breath departed from him, he closed his own eyes; and then
disposed his hands and body into such a posture as required
not the least alteration by those that came to shroud him.'

Thus did John Donne, poet and preacher, pass out of this
life. But the fruit of his gift lives on.

# The Hand of God

There have been many examples, in our modern world, of promising and even very good writers — Rimbaud is of course the most famous — suddenly ceasing to write, giving up abruptly from one day to the next, when nothing in their lives or earlier work could have prepared us for such a move. This is what happened to Victor.

Though only in his early thirties, his career seemed already well-established, his reputation steadily growing. It was not just the quality of what he wrote that drew me to him, but the sheer quantity and variety of it: novels, short stories, poems, articles, stage plays, radio plays, opera libretti — they poured from him in a seemingly endless stream, yet each of them, no matter how small or how great, showed the same qualities of craftsmanship, clarity, precision, wit and fantasy. When one leads a dull and humdrum life, as I do, but has nevertheless had, now and again, intimations of something else of value beyond the purely economic and hedonistic, then a friend like Victor is more than a stimulating companion; he is in some sense a living proof that there is something else to life than merely getting on and getting by. Knowing him, I have sometimes thought, must be what knowing a hero or a saint must have been to the people of an earlier age.

Not that Victor fitted one's common idea of the artist. He lived an ordered, simple life in Clapham, with his wife and daughter, taught in a local school and, even after the relative success of his second and third novels, never showed the least desire to change his way of life. Indeed, he always insisted he needed the regularity of school-teaching, that he did not want to become dependent on his publishers or ever be forced to write what he did not want to write. Nor did he have a very high opinion of publishers and literary people, never accepting invitations to prize-givings, literary festivals or book launches, his own, of course, excepted.

He was not interested in literature; rather, writing was his life. Entering his study at the top of the cool, high-ceilinged house in Clapham, you felt that this was a living, vibrant space, a place of peace and order and creativity. It is impossible to describe it without sounding sentimental or idealistic, so I will only say that on the few occasions when he invited me up and allowed me to sit there with him for a few minutes, I felt at once that my life had been enhanced, and I went away a happier and a richer person for the experience.

That is why when he stopped writing and turned his study into a lumber-room the shock was devastating.

Outwardly, nothing changed. His life went on as it had always done, teaching, being with his family, occasionally inviting friends over and in turn accepting invitations to visit, and to the outsider it would have been impossible to guess that anything dramatic had occurred. His agent and his publisher, though mildly disappointed, were not particularly put out, since his success had always been more a question of esteem than of

large sales, and they had other, more lucrative, authors to whom
to turn. But for me, as the fact sank in that he really did mean
it when he said that he would never write again, it was a blow
almost beyond bearing. I felt when he told me – we were sitting
in the downstairs drawing-room with the French windows open
onto the garden and the sound of birdsong filling the room –
I felt then rather as I imagine clerics must have felt when they
were informed that the new science now proved that the earth
was not the centre of the universe but only a minor planet orbiting
round the sun: It can't be true! Surely someone will arrive soon
to say that it is all a mistake! But it was and no one did.

He was quite open that day about what had happened. It
was not that his gifts had suddenly deserted him. It was not that
he had come to realise that his ambitions would never be
fulfilled. (Such a thought would never have entered his head;
his ambitions were not to win prestigious prizes but to write to
the best of his ability and perhaps to prove himself worthy of
his great heroes, Kleist and Kafka.) No, it was much stranger
than that.

This is what he told me.

He had been sitting at his desk at the top of the house with
the window wide open and the big chestnut almost within
touching distance, his notebook open on the desk in front of
him but his mind far away, when all of a sudden he felt himself
falling. He was quite clear about what was happening, he said.
He was falling out of the study window and he could measure
his descent against the tree. Although he was falling at enormous speed and knew he would hit the ground in a fraction of
a second, he said he was also falling very slowly, every leaf on
the branches of the tree and every cobweb on every leaf and
every ant crawling about the trunk was clearly visible to him

and it seemed to him that he saw them with a clarity and a kind of totality which he had never experienced before.

He knew it was the end, he said, and he knew that somehow he had been expecting this for a long time. That was important, he said: somehow he had been expecting it and even waiting for it for as long as he could remember. He was not frightened, he said, but, on the contrary, calm and lucid and full of a sort of serene acceptance, almost of relief. He reviewed his whole life and concluded that he had done what he could with the gifts and opportunities that he had been given and had no regrets. And it was at that moment, he said, as he was examining his life and recognising it for what it was that he felt a hand fold itself round him and in one swift but firm movement pluck him out of the air and thrust him back through the window and into his chair at the desk in his study.

— It was the hand of God, he said. I had no doubt at all that it was the hand of God. It plucked me out of the air so gently and so firmly, though I was hurtling towards the ground at terrifying speed, and it returned me to where I had been before I began to fall.

— I knew at once that it was the hand of God, he said. And I knew too that everything was over.

— Everything? I said stupidly.

— Everything, he said.

— I don't understand, I said.

— I sat there at my desk, he said, as I had sat only a few minutes, perhaps only a few seconds, earlier. I was quite calm, despite all that had just happened to me. But I knew with absolute certainty that there was no longer any point.

— Any point? I echoed foolishly, for I really did not see what it was he was trying to say.

— The hand of God, he said. It snatched me up. It plucked me out of the air as I was falling. It prevented my certain death. It returned me to my desk as though nothing had happened, as it will always do. Don't you see? he said. It will always snatch me up. Now I am sure of that. However often I fall. It will always ensure that I remain unhurt. That is what is unbearable.

— The world, he went on, has closed in upon me. It is no longer open, as it was before that moment. Now I know that God will always be there ahead of me until the day I die. And without the possibility of falling, really falling, how can I live? How can I write?

I tried to persuade him, of course. I tried to make him see that quite a different construction could be put on those extraordinary events. But he would not have it. Without the possibility of falling, he said, he had lost the possibility of hope. And without the possibility of hope his life, as a man and as a writer, was effectively over.

I changed tack then. Surely, I argued, his experience might have made it necessary, for reasons that I could not fathom, to stop writing temporarily, but there was still life to be lived, still his wife and daughter, his pupils, his friends, his garden, and perhaps one day the urge to write would return.

He looked at me in his familiar way and I sensed that I had not really understood a word of what he had been saying to me. At least I know when I am out of my depth, so that when he said firmly: — We will not speak of it again, please. I simply wanted you to know. — When he said that I could only nod in dumb assent. And, indeed, we have never spoken of it again. His life goes on as before, and so does mine. But we both know that it effectively ended that day when the hand of God plucked him out of the air and returned him to the safety of his desk.

# Tegel

I first saw him there five years ago, when Christa was three. We used to accompany Geoff to the airport because he hated going alone. He said airports were death, though Tegel has always struck me as a friendly place. Friendly but not sad. And I would see him when we went to the airport to wait for Geoff to arrive, from Sarajevo, Athens, Pristina, Moscow, Grozny. Christa didn't ask the usual questions, such as, When is Daddy coming, Mummy? or, Is that Dad's plane, Mummy? She just sat quietly, sucking her thumb and looking at the planes landing and taking off. When Geoff arrived she wouldn't run up to him with happy shouts, as the other children did, she would wait for him to pick her up, her thumb still in her mouth.

Since Geoff has ceased to leave or return, because he no longer lives here with us, she wants nothing better than to go to the airport and sit in the coffee bar and look at the planes landing and taking off. Can we go to the airport today, Mummy? she asks, and if I say no, she turns in on herself and sulks.

One is well insulated in the coffee bar in Tegel. One feels rather than hears the throbbing, the rush, and then the plane is up and away. This is where he sits, in the same corner always, chain-smoking, drinking beer, not looking at the planes but at the air in front of him, lighting one cigarette from another, periodically going to the bar to get another beer. He doesn't look as if he is aware of anything going on around him, but he must be because one day, when the coffee bar was unusually crowded with a party of Japanese and we had been forced to sit at the table next to his, he began to talk as if he knew just who I was. What's happened to your man? he said. The one with the beard. He doesn't live here any more, I said. He began to laugh. He coughed and spluttered, pulled a filthy handkerchief out of his pocket and blew his nose and went on laughing. Once they're up there, he said, when the cough had eventually subsided, why should they ever come down? He turned slowly to face me. It was a mistake to let him go up there into the sky, he said. A mistake in the first place.

I was afraid he would want us to sit near him every time we went into the coffee bar after that, but no, he gave no sign of recognition, sitting staring out into the void, his glass rising regularly to his lips, his bald head and earring shining under the lights, his ponytail laid like a decoration on his shoulder. Occasionally, though, since then, we have talked. He owns a junk shop in Neu-Köln and he comes here when the clutter gets too much for him. I could go anywhere, he says. I dreamed of flying out to Montevideo, to Seattle, to Bangkok. But now the Wall has come down and I could go anywhere, I prefer just to sit here. I drink my coffee and smile, for fear of offending him. Detroit, he says, Buenos Aires. Paris. Tokyo. There are planes to all those places and I have the money to get on board. To get on board, he says, as though that was the most important thing. He has lived in Berlin for the past twenty-five years.

Before that he lived in Magdeburg and worked on the railways. Now he has a junk shop in Neu-Köln. He clears the houses of the dead. There is so much junk piled up in his shop it's impossible to move. His wife left him because the junk got her down. When it gets too much for him he closes up the shop and comes here for a drink and a look at the planes. There is so much room in the sky, he says. It's unbelievable. Unbelievable. When you see those jets taking off you breathe a sigh of relief, he says. They've made it and now they can live up there in their element. Above the clouds. Above the junk. Berlin is like my junk shop in Neu-Köln, he says. You can't move for the clutter. They're trying to clean it up, he says, they're trying to modernise it, but it won't work. The history of Berlin can't just be wiped away, he says. The Wall can't just be wiped away. You've got to integrate the past into the present, he says. You can't just wipe it away or turn it into monuments for tourists as they're trying to do. But everything's too messed up to be integrated, he says. And it's not just Berlin. Look at Naples, Mexico City, Calcutta, he says. I could go to any of those cities but why should I? I don't go anywhere, he says, because once you've been up in the sky why would you ever want to come down? The Nazis wanted to live in Europe as though it was the sky, he says. The Communists wanted to live in Europe as though it was the sky. But it can't be done. All they did was add to the junk, he says. Dead bodies and the remains of the dead. All junk, he says.

When I go and sit with Christa by the window he does not even glance at us. I like that. He knows that if I want to talk I'll come and sit beside him. But I like the window. I can see my reflection in the glass and, beyond it, the aeroplanes landing and taking off. Most of the time the coffee bar is quiet. Hardly a soul comes in here, most people who use the airport don't even

know of its existence, away beyond Gate Three. That's where
I used to sit with Geoff before he went away on one of his
missions, or sit with Christa waiting for him to return. He never
really liked what he was doing. The brutality and the hypocrisy
sickened him. I did it to see if I could, he used to say. What he
really wanted to do was to write. Not ephemeral journalism, he
said, but books. And he could only write books in England. I
need to hear the living language being spoken around me, he
said. I need that if I'm going to be able to write. At first it was
different. I don't belong anywhere, he used to say. I've ended
up in Britain but it might equally well have been France or Italy.
So why not Germany? For a year or two after Christa's birth he
seemed happy in Berlin. He found it invigorating, he said, to be
able to cycle to a concert or a play instead of having to spend
endless hours in buses and tubes. But then something happened.
I don't know what. Or perhaps he was waiting for something
to happen and it didn't. How can one tell? I want to do something with my life, he used to say, and when I replied that he
was already doing something with his life he would laugh and
say, No, no, really do something with it, not this ephemeral
stuff but books, real books. I should have known. Do something with my life – what does that mean except turn in on
yourself, cut yourself off from your ties, ignore the needs and
feelings of others? So now he sits in his room in Kentish Town
doing something with his life – he goes on sending me his books
though he knows I do not read them – and we come to Tegel
and watch the planes. You like them? the man from Neu-Köln
asked me one day, jerking his thumb at the planes. *She* likes them,
I said, taking refuge in the child. Wean her, wean her, he said,
or she won't be fit for anything else. If I could get a ticket that
would keep me up in the skies for the rest of my life, he says,

I'd buy that ticket. Perhaps one day you'll be able to get a ticket to Mars, I say. I don't want to go to Mars, he says. I just want to get away from this junk shop earth. They killed us all taking down the Wall, he says. When it was up we could dream of the other side, now it's down you see there isn't any other side, it's the same shitty junk shop everywhere. He's in a bad mood today, he doesn't usually swear, no matter how many beers he's had, but the next time I come he's sitting in his corner and never even looks at me. I haven't forgotten his words, though. I watch the jets taking off through the reflection of my face. Perhaps he's right about Christa too. Perhaps it's time to wean her from this, to take her to the park and let her play with the other children. The trouble is it's already too late. She won't play with the other children, she only wants to come here. If I take her to the park she sulks and sucks her thumb. I should never have come here with Geoff. I should never have come to wait for Geoff. It's always too late. By the time you realise you shouldn't be doing something you can't not do it any more. That's why Geoff came here to Berlin and that's why he left. The man from Neu-Köln is right, the only escape is in the sky, but the sky's not an option, it's down here we live and perhaps after all Tegel is the only bearable place to be.

# A Glass of Water

There is no pleasanter or more instructive way to spend a morning than to go round an exhibition with Ken. His knowledge of art is so extensive, his eye so good, his feeling for the mood of a picture and of the occasion so assured, that time runs by unnoticed and yet, in retrospect, I find myself returning again and again to this moment of our conversation or that.

Going round the Chardin exhibition with Ken was a particular pleasure. Chardin is a painter we both warm to, but so little that has been written about him seems to correspond in any way to one's experience of those mysterious still lifes, those mysterious still figures. We stood for a long time in front of the 'Glass of Water and Coffee Pot' of 1760. Someone next to us was informing his companion that the painting was all about hierarchy and inversion, and pointing out that the handle of the pot appears to be both turned towards us and seen in profile, 'a veritable feat of the painter's art'. My own thoughts were concerned rather with the strange feeling of peace and wellbeing the picture gave me, even in a crowded gallery on a surprisingly hot spring morning. Ken just said: 'That glass — the water is always fresh, isn't it?'

We stood in front of the 'Girl with Shuttlecock', painted more than twenty years earlier yet unmistakably a product of the same spirit. 'The feathers grow out of her hand,' Ken said, and I saw at once that he was right. And her gaze, which takes in what is before her, is more intently fixed on the secret of her body, so tightly cased around the bust in her plain but elegant dress, yet dreaming of flight. 'That's what all his work is,' Ken said as we moved on, pointing to the spinning top which gives its name to the 'Boy with the Top'. We looked at it in silence.

Afterwards we went back to his place and Esther made us a light lunch. Her hands are always cool. She had not yet seen the show but she has always loved the Chardins in the National Gallery, the incomparable 'House of Cards' and the painting called 'The Lesson', in which a young nurse or older sister takes a child through his first reading exercises, using a knitting needle to point to the words, and the child, barely reaching up to the table, seems to struggle with total concentration to decipher the still mysterious characters. 'I can't imagine seeing sixty works by him in one go,' she said. 'Just concentrate on two or three,' Ken said. 'Forget the others'. He stroked her hand across the table, absent-mindedly. 'Can you do that,' she asked me, 'if the rest are all around you?' 'Not if you don't already know them,' I said. Her eyes are sometimes blue, sometimes green and sometimes violet. It's most disconcerting. 'I could ring Roger,' Ken said, 'and see if he can get you in before the crowds.' She didn't say anything, and we sat round the table like that, with him stroking her white hand and her violet eyes staring into mine. We often sit like that when we have eaten. Sometimes I close my eyes and then I feel her hand in mine, feel nothing but her hand, and then I open them again and see her eyes, see nothing but her eyes. When I have spent a morning at the National

Gallery or at some new show perhaps, at the Hayward or the Royal Academy, it is like a fulfilment of the promises of the day to come home and find that she has made lunch and we sit, practically in silence, holding hands. Often we push the plates aside and sit like that, our legs entwined under the table, looking into each other's eyes. There is no need to speak, and if we speak it is more out of the desire to let our voices float in the air about us than because we have anything to say. I thought today, as I went slowly round the Chardin exhibition at the Royal Academy before going home to her, of the shows I had been round with Ken, and wondered what he would have had to say. It was always so illuminating, such a genuine pleasure, to see a good exhibition with him, but there it is, everything passes, the good and the bad, everything passes.

The house does not feel empty. She fills it with her presence. I wish she had taught me how to make that quiche which was her speciality. I tried to make it once or twice but I must have left out some special ingredient or failed to mix the elements correctly, it always came out heavy and dry, and after a while I gave up. I make myself a salad and, sometimes, if I feel hungry, a soft-boiled egg, and I cut up the toast into fingers as my mother taught me. I do not exactly miss her, though my legs fumble for her under the table if I am not careful, Her presence in the house is particularly strong when I come back from a show, but it is a benign presence. I am filled with her from the soles of my feet to the top of my head and I am particularly aware of her in my chest, as though there was hardly room inside my shirt for the two of us.

Sometimes I leave the meal half-eaten and wander through the house, touching the objects she touched, letting my hand rest on the back of the chair in which she liked to sit. Though there is a little dust on the desk in her study and I stand there making patterns in it with my fingers, no pattern shows, and though I stare into the mirror in the bathroom there is no answering reflection. That is the nature of our condition. It causes me no pain, and, when one comes to think about it, it even has distinct advantages. In a crowded gallery, even on a hot day, I feel no discomfort, experience no constraint. I can concentrate totally on each painting oblivious of the people jostling round me. It is as though I was inside the painting, inside the tight bodice of the little girl with her racket and feathered shuttlecock, inside the hands of the boy looking at the spinning top as they rest casually on the edge of the table, and, yes, inside that glass of water which is always fresh and always present. Everything passes, it tells me, everything passes, including ourselves, and everything is always present.

# Love Across the Borders

— Take your coat, Veronica says to her son as the 11.52 express from Milan glides soundlessly into the main station of Geneva and comes, almost imperceptibly, to a stop. Make sure you haven't forgotten anything.

On the platform she takes his hand: — Can you see a taxi sign anywhere? she asks him.

— There, Mum! he says, swerving off suddenly to the left. Once again she marvels at how big he has grown in the past few months.

In the taxi she gives the driver an address and sits back, peering short-sightedly at the passing houses.

— Are we going to see Philippe? he asks.

— Not now. We're going to the hotel first.

— And then we're going to see him?

— No. Tomorrow morning.

He is silent, playing with his backpack. Then: — Is this Geneva? he asks.

— Yes.

He is silent again.

— I thought we could go for a boat ride on the lake, she says.

Would you like that?

He is silent, staring out of the window.

– Would you? she repeats.

– I don't mind, he says, continuing to gaze out of the window.

– Hotel du Soleil, the driver says, pulling in to the kerb.

\* \* \* \* \*

The next morning, at breakfast, he asks again: – Are we going to see Philippe today?

– Yes, she says.

– Where does he live?

– Not far from here. We'll walk.

In the street she says: – Look, one can see the lake from almost anywhere in this city.

– Come on, she says, stopping and waiting for him. Why are you dawdling so much this morning?

She holds out her hand but he does not take it. He reaches up to my armpit, she thinks, soon he will be up to my shoulder and then he'll be as tall as I am.

She looks at her watch: – We're early, she says. Let's go and have a coffee.

– I don't want a coffee.

– Have a Coke.

Though autumn is drawing in it's still warm enough to sit on the terrace.

– Don't do that, she says as he sucks noisily at the dregs of his Coke through the straw.

He puts the glass down on the table.

– Do you want another? she asks him.

He looks at her in surprise: — Another Coke?

— Why not? she says. We're on holiday, aren't we?

She laughs but he goes on looking at her, puzzled, across the table.

— Or something else? she says. Have whatever you want.

She fumbles in her bag, takes out a packet of cigarettes, selects one, lights it. — What's the matter? she says. What are you looking at me like that for?

— Nothing, he says.

He retreats into himself.

— Go on, she says. Have a milkshake.

— Will you have one?

— No. I don't think so. But why don't you?

— No thank you, he says, in his most adult tone.

— Another Coke then?

— No, Mum, he says. I don't want anything.

She calls for the bill, stubbing out her cigarette as she does so.

Fom her bag she takes a pair of soft black leather gloves. She draws them on, pressing between her fingers, smoothing them over her wrists.

— Do you like them? she asks, holding up her hands for him to see.

— They're all right, he says.

— I think they're very nice, she says.

* * * * *

In the street she takes a piece of paper from her bag, examines it. The boy waits, looking idly round him.

— Come, she says. She pushes him ahead of her.

They round a corner. She says: — Look out for number 52.

He walks beside her. She can feel the heat of his body against her side. — Here, he says.

She presses the buzzer and the door opens. Opposite them is a lift. — Fifth floor, she says.

In the lift she opens her bag and feels about inside it. Then she examines her face in the wall mirror.

The lift stops. The inner doors slide open. She pushes the outer door and they get out.

Three tall doors give on to the landing. She peers at the name on one, moves to the next, peers at the name again, rings the bell.

Silence.

— Come, she says to the boy. Stand here beside me.

She rings again.

Silence.

She waits.

Finally, she says: — All right. We'll come back later.

The lift is still there. She opens the doors and pushes him in ahead of her.

In the street she hesitates a moment, then turns in the direction of the lake.

— What are we going to do? the boy asks.

— We'll have a little walk.

He walks beside her, absently.

They pass a café. — Come, she says. We'll have a drink.

He follows her onto the terrace. She finds a table and sits down.

— What will you have? she asks him.

— Nothing, he says.

— You must have something.

– I'm not thirsty.

– On a hot day like this?

The waiter is standing beside them. She orders a glass of wine for herself and a Coke for the boy. When he returns the waiter makes a great show of opening the bottle and pouring the contents into a long glass half-filled with ice.

The boy stares ahead of him.

– Go on, his mother says, when the waiter has left. Drink up.

She peels off her gloves and lays them on the table beside her.

– I'm not thirsty, the boy says.

– Of course you are. It'll do you good.

– Mum, he says, it's the second one this morning.

– Never mind, she says. This is a special occasion.

Reluctantly, he draws the tall glass towards him and sips the drink through the straw.

She has drunk her wine down. She is examining her face in a pocket mirror she has taken out of her bag. She applies some lipstick.

She returns the lipstick and the mirror to her bag, snaps it shut. – Go on, she says. Drink up.

– I've had enough, the boy says.

She calls the waiter, pays.

She pulls on her gloves and stands up. – Come, she says.

In the street the boy says: – Mum, I need to pee.

– Wait till we get to Philippe's.

– And if he isn't there?

– He'll be there.

They retrace their steps. In the lift mirror she again checks her face. The boy stands beside her, impassive.

Once again she presses the bell. This time, after a pause, there is the sound of footsteps.

The door opens.

The man stares at them in surprise.

— Veronica! he says, when he realises who it is. What are you doing here?

— Are you alone? she asks him.

— Yes, he says, still staring.

— May we come in?

He steps aside. She pushes the boy in ahead of her. — Where's the lavatory? she asks. He needs to go.

He closes the front door behind them. — I'll take him, he says.

When he returns she has gone into the large living-room that gives onto the entrance hall and is standing at the window.

— Veronica, he says, coming towards her. What do you want?

Then he sees the knife in her hand. — No, he says. Veronica. Put that away.

She comes towards him. He reaches out a hand to push her away but she brushes it aside.

— Veronica, he says.

She leans into him and pushes the knife into his stomach as far as it will go. He gasps and sinks onto the sofa, dislodging as he does so a large glass ashtray on the little table by the sofa, which slides to the floor and smashes to pieces. She stands over him, puts her left hand on his shoulder and pulls out the knife. He gasps again and seems to fold in two. She wipes the blade of the knife on his trousers and puts it back in her bag.

The boy is standing at the door.

— Come, she says. We're going.

He stands, looking into the room.

— Philippe's not feeling very well, she says, taking his hand and turning him towards the front door.

In the lift she examines her face in the mirror.

— Come, she says, as they leave the house. We've got to get to the hotel and collect our bags.

She sets off down the street. He trails a few steps behind her.

\* \* \* \* \*

In the train he sits opposite her, staring out of the window.

Finally, he says: — Will we have to go back to Geneva?

— No, she says. I don't think so.

— I'm glad, he says. I didn't like it much, did you?

— I liked the lake, she says.

— I didn't like it much, he says, putting on his most adult expression. It was too pretty-pretty.

She laughs, hearing the expression in his mouth.

— It was, Mum, he says. Didn't you think so?

— I suppose so, she says. Now be quiet. I want to sleep.

# The Two Lönnrots

As Borges lay dying his mind filled with images of lakes, of vast forests of spruce and pine, of an enormous sky. He knew this was Finland, a country he had never visited, but which in these last years had been closer to his heart even than the streets of Buenos Aires in which he had grown up and about which he had written so much and so well. Lönnrot, he thought, and the figure of the poor tailor's son who had risen to become the foremost collector of Finnish folk songs and tales, the Walter Scott, the Brothers Grimm, the Bartok of Karelia, passed before his mind's eye. For it was in the pages of the *Kalevala*, that strange approximation to a national epic put together by Elias Lönnrot after years of wandering and collecting in the north-eastern region of his country, that he had encountered the landscape of Finland which had never afterwards left him, and to which he returned again and again as he had once returned to the pampas and the gauchos of his native land. He had been so taken by this strange man with his strange name that he had appropriated the latter for the hero of one of his most successful stories, 'Death and the Compass'.

At a meeting in an unnamed city of the Third Talmudic

Congress, one of the delegates is found murdered in his room at the Hôtel du Nord. The local police chief, Inspector Treviranus, is in no doubt as to the cause of death: 'No need to look for a three-legged cat here,' he says to his friend and rival, the amateur detective Erik Lönnrot, scourge of the local gangsters. 'We all know that the Tetrarch of Galilee owns the finest sapphires in the world. Someone, intending to steal them, must have broken in here by mistake. Yarmolinsky got up; the robber killed him.' 'Possible, but not interesting,' responds Lönnrot. 'You'll reply that reality hasn't the least obligation to be interesting. I'll answer you that reality may avoid that obligation but that hypotheses may not. In the hypothesis you propose, chance intervenes copiously. Here we have a dead rabbi; I would prefer a purely rabbinical explanation, not the imaginary mischances of an imaginary robber.' Lönnrot's intuition seems to be borne out by the discovery, in the dead rabbi's typewriter, of a piece of paper on which is written: 'The first letter of the Name has been uttered.' Lönnrot takes away with him the dead man's mystical and cabbalistic texts, and gives an interview to a Yiddish journal in which he lays out his hypotheses. Exactly one month later a Jewish hoodlum is found murdered in the western suburbs, and next to his body the message: 'The second letter of the Name has been uttered.' One month after that a man is abducted from a rooming-house in the east of the city where for the past week he has been holed up under an assumed name. Again the message is found: 'The third letter of the Name has been uttered.' Are we dealing here with a campaign to terrify the country's Jews or with some internecine Jewish struggle? Lönnrot is in no doubt that a fourth murder will be committed, since 'the Name' is obviously the tetragrammaton, YHWH, and he predicts the time and place.

A month after the third crime, armed with a map and compass, he makes his way to a mysterious abandoned house, a veritable labyrinth of rooms, corridors and staircases in the southern sector of the city. There he is apprehended by the master criminal Red Scharlach, who proceeds to explain to him how, to take revenge for Lönnrot's role in the incarceration of his brother, he has set about entrapping him. The first crime was indeed an accident, as Inspector Treviranus had suspected: one of Red Scharlach's men, having decided to double-cross the organisation and steal the jewels of the Tetrarch himself, and having blundered into the wrong room, was surprised by the rabbi, who had stayed up late to type his notes for an essay he was preparing on the names of God; he had no option but to kill him. Scharlach, learning through the papers of Lönnrot's subtle hypothesis, and of the note found in the typewriter, decided it would be both poetic and expedient to kill two birds with one stone. He had the traitor murdered and clues left to lead Lönnrot to the conclusion he wished him to arrive at; then he disguised himself and holed up in the rooming-house, from which he had his men 'abduct' him. 'I interspersed repeated signs that would lead you, Lönnrot, the reasoner, to understand that the series was quadruple... I have premeditated everything, Erik Lönnrot, in order to attract you to the solitude of Triste-le Roy.' Then, taking careful aim, he fires the bullet which kills the sleuth.

What has all this to do with Finland and the *Kalevala*? What has Lönnrot the detective to do with Lönnrot the collector of folk songs? Everything and nothing, thought Borges as he lay dying. Everything because nothing. He had always understood that he could not and should not try to speak the skies and streams, the lakes and forests of the world. He had always sensed

that, because description is always lame, writing must take
another direction if it is to be of interest to the writer and the
reader. The rules of realism are too lax to be a challenge to the
true writer, he had always felt, for it does not take much to
imitate chance and of what possible interest could anyone find
the series of coincidences which form the building blocks of
most novels? On the other hand, 'the interesting', while the stuff
of true Art, becomes, in the real world, not only dangerous but
positively inimical to life. For it seeks to turn life itself, in all
its glorious randomness, into pattern and meaning, and that way
lies madness and not only madness, if the history of the twen-
tieth century is anything to go by, but unspeakable disaster. For
what else lay behind the megalomaniacal actions of Hitler and
Stalin but the desire to turn the contingent into the necessary,
to force the world to conform to their imaginations? That is
why, at the end of what he had always felt was his best story,
the hero, to escape the seductive power of the imaginary, retires
to a quiet hotel in Adrogué to pursue the mundane but exacting
task of translating Thomas Browne's *Urne Burial* into Quevedan
Spanish. Let the artist, he thought, not try to take the place of
God, for that is the ambition of madmen and power-crazy
tyrants; let him instead know precisely what his own place is
and, from that place, seek to convey to the reader a sense of all
that lies beyond the realm of art, the realm of the imagination,
let him seek to convey in this way a sense of the unspeakable
fields and lakes and clouds, of the unspeakable wonder of our
common world. He thought: the two Lönnrots, the real one
and the fictive one, are the secrets of my life and work. I have
been the second Lönnrot, the suicidal detective, the creator of
imaginary labyrinths, but I would really like to have been the
other, a collector, if not a singer, of songs. And in my best work,

he thought, the work by which I will live on, as Elias Lönnrot lives on in the pages of the *Kalevala*. I have perhaps managed to make the relations between them manifest.

And with that thought he died.

# He Contemplates a Photograph
## in a Newspaper

It takes time to look at an image.

He spreads the paper flat on his desk and leans over it to try and get a better view of the small black and white photograph in the top right-hand corner which has caught his attention.

What he first sees is a woman, standing in a wood or forest in the sunlight. It seems to be spring or early summer, for the leaves are out, but not so thickly as to hide the branches, the trunks. The woman is young and sturdy, and, from what one can see of her, rather beautiful. She stands sideways to the camera, looking off to the right, her features hidden by her abundant glossy hair, cropped at the shoulders. Next to her, the only mass of black in the entire image, stands the misshapen trunk of a large tree whose branches are cut off by the top edge of the photo.

The sunlight plays on the woman's back as she stands, looking off to the right. A sense of peace pervades the scene.

What is she looking at? Her right arm hangs at her side, yet her hand is held slightly away from her and her fist appears to be clenched, though it is difficult to see clearly as a leafy sapling half hides it. She is wearing a sweater of some light colour and a white skirt, smooth around the buttocks, pleated below, which barely reaches to her knees. The light catches the back of her strong shapely legs and her bare feet, the left foot half-hidden by the right. Her heels are slightly higher than her toes, though she does not appear to be straining as she would be if she were standing on tiptoe.

Some images exude noise, others silence. Here the sense is of utter silence in the forest, utter peace, with only the sunlight, the trees and the solitary woman.

Beneath her feet, more leaves. Yet she does not appear to be standing on a bed of leaves. In fact, as he looks more closely, he sees that there is a small but distinct gap between the woman's heels and the floor of the forest. Suddenly, sickeningly, he understands what it is he is looking at. The woman is not standing at all. She is hanging from a branch of the dark misshapen tree, although the rope from which she hangs is lost in the sunlight, the leaves and the branches, while her abundant glossy hair hides the noose about her neck.

Now that he understands what it is he is seeing he can sense how the body would move, turning a little this way and that in the breeze, if there is a breeze in this silent, sunlit wood.

Only now does he read the caption: 'A refugee from Srebrenica who hanged herself after the Serb capture of the town.'

# Heart's Wings

It was her favourite passage. She was never as fond of Latin as she was of Greek literature and never, as far as I know, read any other work of Ovid's. But she loved the *Metamorphoses* and few pieces of literature moved her as much as the story of Ceyx and Alcyone in Book XI. I had brought home John Frederick Nims's 1965 reprint of Arthur Golding's 1567 translation of the *Metamorphoses*, knowing her fondness for sixteenth-century poetry, her feeling that even the wonders of seventeenth-century English verse constituted a decline from the clarity, the innocence of the earlier period, an intrusion of the self which was to ruin European poetry in her eyes till it rediscovered its roots in the work of Yeats and Stevens and Montale. But I had not expected her to respond to it with quite the enthusiasm she did. After that Ovid for her was Golding (though I tried to interest her in some modern translations) and the best of Ovid was the story of Ceyx and Alcyone.

What was it about the story and its telling that moved her so? Fierce Daedalion and his gentle brother Ceyx are the sons of Lucifer, the morning star. Daedalion's beautiful daughter is wooed by both Hermes and Apollo and bears each a son. But her good fortune goes to her head. Rashly, she boasts that she is superior in every way to Diana and the incensed goddess shoots her dead for her presumption. Her father, mad with grief, flings himself from Parnassus but Apollo takes pity on him and transforms him into a bird, a fierce hawk, to reflect his warlike nature.

Ceyx, meanwhile, has married Alcyone, the daughter of Aeolus, the god of the winds. Now, disturbed by his brother's fate, he decides to consult an oracle, not the one at Delphi, which is close at hand but access to which is dangerous, since the road is infested with robbers, but the more distant oracle of Claros, best reached by sea. Alcyone pleads with him not to go, reminds him that the sea is even more dangerous than the land and that she, as the daughter of Aeolus, knows all about the unpredictability of the winds, their ability to arise suddenly and to destroy even the largest ship. If he is determined to set sail then let him at least take her with him; like that they will undergo danger together and if necessary die together. But Ceyx will not hear of it. If I go now, he says, I will be home in two months, don't force me to delay. Unwillingly, she gives in. She accompanies him down to the beach, watches him board the vessel, and the two wave goodbye to each other, she from the shore, he from the stern, until they can see each other no longer. But she goes on gazing at the receding ship until it disappears over the horizon.

At first all goes well, as a pleasant breeze wafts them on their journey. But soon the breeze changes into a wind which grows more and more fierce. The sky darkens, the waves billow and in no time at all the ship is being tossed on a stormy sea with the waves crashing against its sides. The sailors try to cope:

> Sum haalde asyde the Ores:
> Sum fensed in the Gallyes sydes, sum down the
>                                   sayleclothes rend:
> Sum pump the water out, and sea to sea ageine doo send.
> Another hales the sayleyards downe. And while they did
>                                   eche thing
> Disorderly, the storm increast, and from each quarter fling
> The wyndes with deadly foode,* and bownce the raging
>                                   waves togither.

At last the ship can take no more. The mast breaks, the waters pour in, and it sinks to the bottom. Clinging to a piece of wreckage, Ceyx calls out to his father Lucifer, to his father-in-law Aeolus, and to his beloved wife. All in vain. As he goes under he is still uttering Alcyone's name, praying that his body may be washed ashore so that 'by her most loving handes he might be layd in grave'. That day, says the poet, 'Lightsum Lucifer' was dim, hidden in mourning behind dark clouds.

Alcyone, knowing nothing of this, has been praying daily to the gods to bring her husband home safely, but this soon starts to embarrass Juno, who knows that the time for such prayers is long past. She arranges for a dream to come to Alcyone to inform her of the awful truth. In due course, as she lies sleeping, Morpheus appears at her bed's head in the form of her husband, 'Pale, wan, stark nakt, and like a man that was but lately deade', dripping wet from head to foot. He recounts what has happened to him and begs her to rise up, put on her mourning garments and perform the proper rituals. 'Let me not to Limbo go/ Unmoorned for', he says. She tries to embrace

* _feud_

him, but her arms close round empty air. 'Tarry!' she cries out, 'whither flyste? together let us go.' Her own voice wakes her and now she begins to lament in earnest, striking her cheeks with her fists, pulling out her hair, tearing her robe from her breast. I begged you not to leave me, she says to him, but you would not listen. How much better it would have been for us to die together, not to have been divided as we are now. As it is, 'Already, absent in the waves now tossed have I bee. / Already have I perished. / And yit the sea hath thee / Without mee.' I cannot go on living, she says, at least in death there is a sense in which we will be together once more, for 'Although in tumb the bones of us togither may not couch, / Yit in a graven Epitaph my name thy name shall touch.'

It is morning. She leaves the house and makes for the seashore, the place by the jetty where she had watched his boat depart. As she gazes out to sea, recalling every detail of that day, something catches her eye. She looks more closely and sees that it is the body of a man, rolling in the swell. Her heart goes out in pity for him and for the wife he has left behind, and then, suddenly, she recognises it: it is her husband, Ceyx: 'Then plainely shee did see/ And know it, that it was her feere. She shreeked, It is he.' Clambering on to the jetty, she rushes along it till she is just above the body, then hurls herself off the parapet into the sea.

But she never falls. Instead, she skims the surface like a seabird on new-found wings. Uttering plaintive cries she settles on the body and tries to embrace it with her rough bill. Perhaps in response to this, or perhaps because of some movement of the waves, Ceyx lifts up his face to her, and in a moment he too has been transformed into a bird and is flying over the sea beside her. Together they loved, says the poet, and together they suffered, no parting followed them in their new-found form. They mate, have young, and in the winter season, for seven days of calm, Alcyone broods over her nest on the surface of the waters while her father Aeolus reins in the winds and holds the waters smooth for the sake of his descendants.

What was it about the story and its telling that moved her so? She had lost her father when she was five and her mother when she was ten. Though she found it painful to talk about it, she had told me about it often enough, but while she was alive I somehow never made the imaginative effort to understand what this might have meant to her. After all, she was my mother, she was old and wise and there to comfort and protect me when I was troubled or in pain. The thought that she could herself be wounded and sorrowing, while I could understand it intellectually, I was never able to grasp emotionally. But now she is dead everything is different. I reread the story and try to enter her mind as she read. Of course there is no need to search for autobiographical explanations as to why certain works of art move us: there are thousands of reasons, we all know what loss and sorrow entail, we can all enter the world of those who are bereaved. And yet I cannot help feeling that this passage, out of all the myriad stories which make up the *Metamorphoses*, moved her so because it spoke to her own experience.

As she grew older she grew more fearful. She, who had ensured our survival in France during the war; who had taken the decision, at forty-five, to leave the Egypt where she was born and where she had family and friends, for a foreign country where she did not even know if she would be allowed to settle, simply because she felt that that was necessary for my education; who had worked uncomplainingly through her thirties and forties at menial jobs to see me through school and university

— she began, in her seventies and eighties, to dread being abandoned. Even a trip of a few days on my part filled her with
anxiety — for me, for herself. She tried to hide it, knowing that
I would take this as an attempt on her part to tie me down and
so grow resentful, but she had never been good at hiding her
emotions and in a way I loved her for that, though I did indeed
resent that particular manifestation of it. It was then, I think,
as she grew older and frailer, more and more reliant on me for
the simplest practical things, but also shorn of the mental
toughness which had seen her — and me — through so much —
it was then that the demons she had fought so successfully to
keep at bay all her life returned to lay siege to her body and
mind. It was then she began to feel again the terror of betrayal
which first her father's illness and death, and then her mother's
illness and death had instilled into her, and which she had
managed to overcome for so long. Her husband's abandonment
of her, pregnant and with a two-year-old child, in the middle
of the war, can only have added to that, and the subsequent
death, after only a few days, of her second child, must have
finally convinced her, at some deep inarticulate level, that
nothing she loved could be held for long. Our subsequent life
together gave her a new happiness and a new strength, of course,
but then, as the years went by and she grew more and more
reliant on me, she must have felt that if she lost me it would
simply be more than she could bear.

   Books are strange things. The mark of a classic is that it can
speak afresh to each generation, and Ovid's *Metamorphoses* has
been doing that since the book first saw the light of day. It spoke
to Chaucer, who retold the story of Ceyx and Alcyone, dwelling
on Iris's trip to the cave of the god of sleep, in the first part of
his first major poem, *The Book of the Duchess*, which I had sent to

her from Oxford shortly after reading it, but which evoked little
response from her then. It spoke to Arthur Golding in the
sixteenth century and to Shakespeare and to Pound and Eliot.
In the Golding translation it spoke to her, in particular the story
of Ceyx and Alcyone. Across all those centuries, across the
barriers of language and culture, via a simple little tale of how
the kingfisher came – as the ancients thought – to make her
nest in the sea, she found her pain renewed and at the same time
made bearable because spoken by another and spoken in memo-
rable language: the language Ovid used and the language a
sixteenth-century English translator used to turn the Latin into
his own tongue. And now I too, as I try to come to terms with
her death, read and take comfort from those words. Why?
Partly because by reading what she herself read and loved I feel
closer to her and she lives for me a little. And partly because of
the story itself and the way it is told. For this is a tale as firmly
rooted in the real as anything in Homer or the Bible. When
King David says, about the son God has taken from him in
punishment for his adultery with Bathsheba and his complicity
in the murder of her husband: 'Can I bring him back again? I
shall go to him, but he shall not return to me', the painful
acknowledgement of a hard truth has something satisfying and
even purgative about it. Yes, we think, that is how it is, I shall
go to him, but he will not return to me. That is the law of life
and it is good to have it stated so simply and so well. And when
Homer, speaking of Castor and Pollux, the two brothers whom
their sister Helen thinks to be still alive and either in the Greek
camp or back home in the country of their birth, says: No, she
was wrong, for 'her brothers lay / motionless in the arms of
life-giving earth, long dead / in Lakedaimon of their fathers',
he is not only giving the listener information, not only giving

us an example of what scholars call epic irony, but saying something profound about death itself: Helen's brothers are now
buried in the earth and she will never see them again, but the
earth itself is life-giving, the source of all food, and they are
after all buried where they would wish to be, in their dear native
land. Death is part of a larger rhythm and we would do well to
recognise and accept that, though this does not mean that we
should not sorrow and lament the death of a loved one.

Ovid's account is not so very different. He too recognises
the finality of death. Ceyx and Alcyone will never be reunited
in any of the senses in which we, in this life, can understand the
term, for death changes everything, both for the person who has
died and the one who survives. It is the ultimate metamorphosis.
What lends the story its special poignancy, what she responded
to when she first read it and what I now respond to as I reread
it in the wake of her death, is the perception of the role of the
grieving and longing heart: as Alcyone leaps from the jetty in
despair she suddenly takes flight, and that flight is the literal
expression of the heart's leap into oneness with the loved and
lost person. It is her desire to be with him which transforms
her: the wings of the heart and the wings of metamorphosis are
one and the same. But the fact of metamorphosis underlines the
hard truth that as their old selves they will never again be
together:

> And with her crocking neb then growen to slender bill
> and round,
> Like one that wayld and moorned still shee made a
> moaning sound.

There is a further truth. The wings of the heart are also the wings of the imagination: as we read we enter into Alcyone's sorrow and loss and then into her miraculous gain, and we live it even as we recognise that it is possible only in the imagination.

Alcyone's story has been prepared for by the fate of Daedalion, but in his case, though Apollo takes pity on him 'and on the soodaine as hee hung / Did give him wings', he turns into the fierce and warlike creature he always was: a bird of prey. Ceyx and Alcyone, on the other hand, having once known the calm of a deep and trusting love are transformed, after the anguish of separation, tempest, death, dream and lamentation, into birds of calm, bringing peace even to the sea in the midst of winter storms:

> And now Alcyon sitts
> In wintertime upon her nest, which on the water flitts
> A sevennight. During all which tyme the sea is calme and
> still,
> And every man may to and from sayle saufly at his will.

Sacha went to her death in some physical pain after weeks of petty torment, but at the end she was at peace. She found the strength to call me to her and tell me she was tired of her body and felt the time had come to let it go. 'I have no fear of death,' she said. 'I know it is the end. I want you to know that you made the second part of my life as happy as it is possible to be.' Reading Ovid's story I think again of that moment, but without pain, rather with a kind of pride and a sense of peace: heart's wings.